A SHOT IN THE DARK

SPEED

THE DEEP

CELEBRATING CINEMA.

In the art of film-making, it's the smallest details that bring a world to life. Only when every detail is just right can the audience be truly immersed. Rolex is proud to recognise the art and craft of film-making, and to have been a part of some of cinema's most iconic moments. It doesn't just tell time. It tells history.

OYSTER PERPETUAL DATEJUST 41

ROLEX

Like no place that ever was.

sundance

MOUNTAIN RESORT

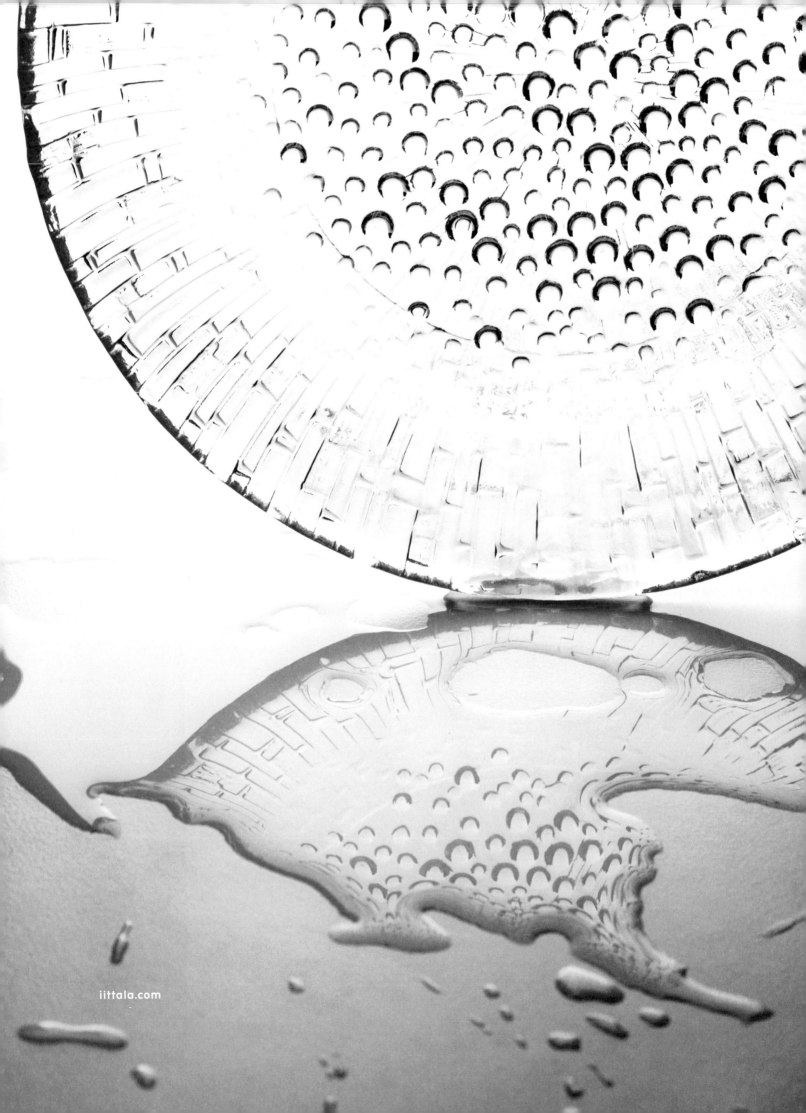

The Kinfolk Entrepreneur explores how visionary ideas take root and ripen into successful businesses, whether they are established on the strength of a single vision, brought about by the power of a partnership or serve to create communities. Join Nathan Williams and the *Kinfolk* team as they visit more than 40 entrepreneurs around the world and explore the myriad ways in which the pursuit of meaning and passion, and the experiences of disappointment and defeat, can motivate professional success. Featuring insightful interviews with leaders from the worlds of publishing, architecture, fashion, design and beyond, *The Kinfolk Entrepreneur* captures the ambitions and realities of today's creative class and offers tips, advice and inspiration for anyone hoping to forge their own professional path.

"*Becoming a successful entrepreneur extends beyond the strength of one's ideas and the ability to profit from them.*"

NATHAN WILLIAMS

KINFOLK

FOUNDER & CREATIVE DIRECTOR
Nathan Williams

EDITOR-IN-CHIEF
Julie Cirelli

EDITOR
John Burns

BRAND DIRECTOR
Amy Woodroffe

DESIGN DIRECTOR
Alex Hunting

ART DIRECTION
Molly Mandell
Kevin Pfaff

CEO
Peter Hildebrandt

COMMUNICATIONS DIRECTOR
Jessica Gray

CASTING DIRECTOR
Sarah Bunter

SALES & DISTRIBUTION DIRECTOR
Frédéric Mähl

ADVERTISING DIRECTOR
Pamela Mullinger

COPY EDITOR
Rachel Holzman

STUDIO MANAGER
Aryana Tajdivand-Echevarria

CONTRIBUTING EDITORS
Michael Anastassiades
Jonas Bjerre-Poulsen
Andrea Codrington Lippke
Ilse Crawford
Margot Henderson
Leonard Koren
Hans Ulrich Obrist
Amy Sall
Matt Willey

ILLUSTRATION
Chidy Wayne

STYLING, HAIR & MAKEUP
Sue Choi
Paul Frederick
Lucy-Ruth Hathaway
David Lamb
Lela Maloney
Lyz Marsden
Kenneth Pihl Nissen
David Nolan
Mike O'Gorman
Rebecca Rojas
Kristen Ruggiero
Sabina Vitting Simmelhag
X. Valverde

**PRODUCTION, STYLING
& SET DESIGN**
Kim Hallsworth
Joanna Goodman
Samantha McCurdy
Sandy Suffield
Samuel Åberg

PUBLICATION DESIGN
Alex Hunting

WORDS
Shireen Ahmed
Alex Anderson
Ellie Violet Bramley
Matt Castle
MacKenzie Lewis Kassab
Charmaine Li
Harriet Fitch Little
Jessica Lynne
Sarah Moroz
Sala Elise Patterson
David Plaisant
Asher Ross
Tristan Rutherford
Charles Shafaieh
Pip Usher
Molly Young

PHOTOGRAPHY
Jonas Bjerre-Poulsen
Rodrick Bond
Robin Broadbent
Pelle Crépin
Sean Davidson
Tigre Escobar
Marion Ettlinger
Elizabeth Felicella
Emma Hartvig
Bruna Kazinoti
Stephen Kugler
Gabby Laurent
Katie McCurdy
Jacopo Moschin
Mark Sanders
John and Chris Schoonover
Anders Schønnemann
Aaron Tilley
Marsý Hild Þórsdóttir
Pia Winther

info@kinfolk.com
www.kinfolk.com

Published by Ouur Media
Amagertorv 14, Level 1
1160 Copenhagen, Denmark

The views expressed in Kinfolk magazine are those of the respective contributors and are not necessarily shared by the company or its staff.

SUBSCRIBE
Kinfolk is published four times a year. To subscribe, visit kinfolk.com/subscribe or email us at info@kinfolk.com

CONTACT US
If you have questions or comments, please write to us at info@kinfolk.com. For advertising inquiries, get in touch at advertising@kinfolk.com

Pixel 2

Starters

"Music requires more freedom than design. It can't be perfect."
KILO KISH – P. 51

SCHOOLHOUSE

ELECTRIC & SUPPLY CO.™

Portland | New York | Pittsburgh (Summer 2018)

schoolhouse.com | #schoolhouseliving

"Art is like sex. If you don't relax, you won't enjoy it."
SIRI HUSTVEDT – P. 179

Photograph: Pelle Crépin

LEVI'S®
MADE & CRAFTED®

ARTFUL CONSTRUCTION. ELEVATED DETAILS.
LEVI'S® BY DESIGN.

RAINS

Drip, drip, drip.

rains.com

Welcome

As we developed this volume of *Kinfolk*, across the United States athletes were using their tremendous visibility to draw attention to racial inequality, discrimination and the disproportionately high rate of police violence against people of color. By taking a knee or raising a fist, these athletes peacefully and powerfully demonstrated courage in the face of oppression. In direct opposition to those in power who attempted to silence and distort their message, they lifted those around them, used their platform to advocate for the voiceless and held American society to a higher standard.

Bravery is the essence of sport: To play, to fight, to challenge the body and the mind— these are the seemingly ordinary activities that can elevate even the most uneventful of days. More and more do sport, exercise and fitness play a central role in modern life. Socially, they are a fomenting agent for community-building, activism and change. On an individual level, they are forces for enriching one's inner life and bolstering self-esteem. Our special sports section explores the values that underpin an active life: camaraderie and self-discipline, joy, endurance, balance and leisure.

On page 137, Alex Anderson examines some of the modern precedents for political activism in sport. He addresses the now-iconic image of Olympians Tommie Smith and John Carlos receiving their medals with bowed heads and raised fists as well as the early victories of Dutch runner Fanny Blankers-Koen, who battled sexism throughout her career. "Sport enacts larger political conflicts," Anderson writes. "World-class athletes become both spirited performers and fierce partisans— proxy warriors whose successes or failures reverberate far beyond the field of competition". On page 130, David Sedaris, in an excerpt from The New Yorker, uses humor to lampoon the obsession-inducing grip of activity trackers. "Why is it some people can manage a thing like a Fitbit, while others go off the rails and allow it to rule, and perhaps even ruin, their lives?" he asks, as he sails past his Fitbit's 10,000-step-a-day quota. "At the end of my first sixty-thousand-step day, I staggered home with my flashlight knowing that I'd advance to sixty-five thousand, and that there will be no end to it until my feet snap off at the ankles."

In rural England, we meet Amanda Brooks— an American former fashion director now pursuing a sporting life among the rolling hills of the Cotswolds. On page 162, Harriet Fitch Little puts the cult of contemporary wellness and clean eating into context with a potted history of bad dieting advice, and on page 138, we examine how language and metaphor shape the way we view sport and the human body.

Elsewhere in the issue, we chart the emergence of Kilo Kish, whose distinctive pop sound is reflective of a new generation of musicians using design, language and art as lenses for interpreting music. We trace the legacy of Gordon Parks, a pioneer in photojournalism and fashion photography; attend a Surrealist-inflected dinner party hosted by photojournalist turned cook and entertainer Lee Miller; dig through the archives of Donald Judd's Marfa library; polish off the brief history of spoons and forks; and marvel at the "smupidity" of modern society ("The mental state," according to Hans Ulrich Obrist, "where we acknowledge that we've never been smarter as individuals, and yet somehow we've never felt stupider.").

JULIE CIRELLI & JOHN CLIFFORD BURNS

Multiroom speakers that complement your home

URBANEARS

www.urbanears.com

1
Starters

ASHER ROSS

Everything and Nothing

It was *Isaac Newton* who suggested that black was not a color. History suggests otherwise.

True black has no hue; it represents the complete absence or absorption of color. It is, to human eyes, the most common thing in the universe, and we have made it a color all its own.

Nothing is older than black in mythological and religious lore. To scientists, it was there, alone, in the incomprehensible non-being that preceded the Big Bang. The primordial Greek deities Nyx (night) and Erebus (darkness) were preceded only by Chaos. The Hindu goddess Kali, worshipped as the "mother of the universe," takes her name from the Sanskrit word for black. The Abrahamic religions also gave darkness its due. "Let there be light," said the Lord in the Old Testament, and the primal void was illuminated: "And the light shineth in darkness, and the darkness comprehended it not."

Black has long been in fashion. It is the color of the timeless little black dress, and of Holly Golightly's cigarette holder. Queen Victoria draped it on in regal luxury, whereas the Puritans, finding no bleaker option, cut from it their stoic uniform. Black were the hats of Dutch bankers and spaghetti western antiheroes. Black is the color of the dominatrix's crop, and of every last umbrella at an English funeral.

Alex Berggruen, a specialist in Post-War & Contemporary Art at Christie's, and head of the department's Afternoon Sale, notes that black plays a number of structural roles in the history of painting, whether in the horrifying gloom of Goya's *Saturn Devouring His Son*, or in the mesmerizing topography of Rauschenberg's *Black Paintings*. He notes, "Black, as a color, was not really used by the impressionists, yet after them the cubists took a more sober, more somber approach. They embraced black as a sacred color, and used it in the service of multidimensionality, ushering it into the age of early modernism."

Berggruen recalls a pivotal encounter with black that occurred early on in his career at Christie's, when he had the opportunity to privately research and examine *Guitare et Rhum* by the pioneering cubist George Braque. The painting, composed on a black, ovoid canvas, renders a guitar and a bottle of rum in arresting geometry. "Cubism had a lot to do with seeing elements from the world, whether a still life, a mountain or a figure, at different angles, and then implementing those different angles into a composition all at once," Berggruen says. "And the power of black, in consort with the elements of the foreground, allows these things to pop out and be appreciated."

It is easy to associate black with endings, but in Berggruen's eyes, it is an alchemical force that can reveal things in their fullest. He quotes a portion of a letter from Braque, "...I'm now doing my canvases on a black background... it's a color that we've been deprived of for so long by Impressionism and is so beautiful."

Lick the Knife

Memorable moments from the history of flatware.

While the merits of the silver-plated bonbon scoop, many-tined cake breaker and gilded potato chip server are debatable, the spoon, knife and fork remain ubiquitous across many cultures.

From the Anglo-Saxon *spon* meaning *chip*, the spoon has for millennia come in myriad forms, including animal horn, shell and wood. Today, we also see more conceptual designs such as metal made to look like hand-carved flint tools in the Sekki collection conceived by Japanese designer Nendo.

The fork, however, has not enjoyed such easy or universal acceptance. In 1004, according to lore, Maria Argyropoulina, the niece of the Byzantine emperor, brought gold forks with her when she married the Venetian doge's son. Their use prompted censure by a priest, who declared, "God in his wisdom has provided man with natural forks—his fingers." The tool, initially two-tined and now three, gained popularity centuries later in part due to Louis XIV banning pointed knives (used for piercing food) at the table to curb violence. In the early 20th century, the futurists tried abolishing forks and knives altogether. The too-traditional utensils clashed with their zeal for "modern" experiences that emphasized audacity, danger and general revolt. More tactile, sensory-engaging instruments were better than the current models, which they argued no longer required our conscious thought or attention.

The Amsterdam-based artist collective Steinbeisser (German for *biting on rock*) may be closest in realizing this dining vision. For their "experimental" culinary events, the group inverts the rule of form following function. So chefs take their direction from the utensils designed for the meal by numerous international artists. Opera glasses and mini-tripods are among the objects that have been converted into tableware. Another object required multiple diners working together to bring food to mouth. Beyond creating an entertaining evening, Steinbeisser hopes the experiences—which demand slowing down the act of eating and depending on others' assistance—will accentuate food's power of bringing people together.

FULL SCOOP
by Charles Shafaieh

The ice cream knife and scythe-like silver-plated servers used in France and the overly complicated scoops favored in America were replaced in 1897 by the "ice cream mold and disher" patented by Alfred L. Cralle—the first African-American to receive a solo invention patent. A conical or domed device with a deep barrel and mechanical lever that swiped along the back of the basin and released the frozen confection, Cralle's tool prevented ice cream from sticking to the scoop. His still-popular design made serving so simple that it may well have contributed to the rise in consumption, prompting a German officer in World War I to say about America: "We do not fear that nation of ice cream eaters." *Top: Alessi 380 ice cream scoop. Middle: Alison Jackson tea scoops. Bottom: Hay Clip Clip scoop.*

Enduring Love

Advice on producing a perennially popular classic.

To Kill A Mockingbird is a perennial seller, but Harper Lee's estate has attempted to control its legacy following her death, radically altering its publishing plan and withdrawing it from mass-market production.

Did you see *Teen Wolf Too*? No? Well, I'll save you the bother. It was similar to werewolf-beats-bullies-and-falls-in-love flick *Teen Wolf*, but with no discernible storyline and the subtle exclusion of Michael J. Fox. It was awful. IMDb gave it a score of 3.2 and that was being generous. Needless to say, the movie is not considered a classic.

However, some of its peers are classics. Eighties blockbusters like *Aliens* and *Dirty Dancing* are probably being shown today on one of the myriad channels your television or device has access to. Works of literature like *Romeo and Juliet* and *The Great Gatsby* still sell in the thousands, despite being free on the internet. So, why do some works of art have an unlimited shelf life, while others go straight to DVD?

Entrepreneur Ryan Holiday, author of the book *Perennial Seller*, has distilled the essence of pop longevity into a formula for perpetual renown. He helps songwriters, filmmakers and authors bang out classics that will still be popular in 20 years' time. It's all about "timeless concepts," according to Holiday. "While *Star Wars* was a cutting-edge sci-fi movie when it came out in 1977, it was also deliberately rooted in the timeless concept of the 'hero's journey'." Forty years on, its enduring popularity is evidenced by the sequels and prequels still being made today.

Harper Lee's *To Kill a Mockingbird* follows the same model. It's all about "the triumph of values," concludes Holiday. "There's a reason that Lee's editor sent *Go Set a Watchman* back for edits—it didn't nail those timeless concepts."

In the musical realm, Holiday has an altogether more Hollywood technique to ensure a lasting number. "You should do what Max Martin does (the songwriter behind hits by Adele, Taylor Swift and the Backstreet Boys). He tests the music out in a convertible on an oceanfront road. It does the job if the song entertains, and captures what it means to feel free."

SARAH MOROZ

Mona Omar

A discussion about diversifying body standards and the power of visibility in fashion.

Photograph: Anders Schønnemann, Styling: Kenneth Pihl Nissen, Hair and Makeup: Sabina Vitting Simmelhag

Mona Omar is a Copenhagen-based art director just starting her career. She began contributing creative direction to the lookbooks for Baserange—a Danish line of sustainably made undergarments and leisurewear basics—after an unexpected encounter with the label's founder. Over several seasons, she has helped articulate the brand's progressive aesthetic, which celebrates female comfort and body diversity. Omar, actively inspired by her parents' East African roots and their quest to improve the world, aims to influence new norms of representation.

To start, tell me a bit about your background. I grew up in the suburbs of Copenhagen, in a family of modern-day rebels. My parents came to Denmark as refugees from Somalia in the '80s when they were young adults. My father worked for the NGO Save the Children, and my mother is a teacher and the founder of an organization that combats female genital mutilation. As a child, I always wanted to have a "save-the-world" kind of job.

How did you gravitate toward design and fashion? It was a mere coincidence. I was at a restaurant and Marie-Louise Mogensen, the founder of Baserange, and the photographer Dan McMahon were lurking by the entrance. They were creeping around and looking at me so much that I thought I had taken their seats. They eventually came over and said that they wanted to feature me in their lookbook. A week later I was at the shoot. Afterward, we started working together. I don't spend much time contemplating fashion or even design. My work is mostly based on the idea of a better world, stories and narratives, and representation. But I like to look good.

What were you working on prior? I was at university for international studies and communication. Before that, I was working on a manuscript. I'm trying to figure out how to tell a story about something real yet constructed, which has immediate truth and honesty. I've put it on pause.

In terms of art direction, what is key for you to convey about women in general? Stories that we haven't heard before, or bodies that we haven't seen before, matter.

How do you find these important narratives and silhouettes? I look for something I don't usually see, something absent in mainstream and Western-dominated standards of beauty, especially when it comes to bodies. You would want to hear these stories if the subjects wanted to tell you. You meet people, and you talk and talk and talk, and it's so beautiful to get to know someone directly from their heart through their mouth. It's so intimate. I like being so close to someone I don't know.

Baserange is clear about its sustainable approach to production and design. What do you think can be done to institute better practices in the fashion industry at large? Everyone should feel a responsibility for sustainability and a better world. That would ensure better practices. I see a lack of transparency and honesty from brands toward their consumers. They deserve to know at what cost they're buying something so that they can choose otherwise, or at least know what they are buying. Like the trend you see in the world of gastronomy—with the focus on local and seasonal produce, strong relationships between farmers, restaurants and guests—the fashion consumer should be able to trace a garment back to its materials, chemicals, places and people. Ultimately, it's way bigger than just this industry. The question of consumerism as a burning global issue is a mainstay.

Who are some muses or icons you admire for their look? I admire a lot of people for breaking barriers by just walking out the door in the morning and being themselves, despite facing a hostile world.

Deciphering the limits of self-improvement.

Photograph: Chris Schoonover and Jonathan Schoonover, Styling: Lela Maloney

CHARMAINE LI

Against Perfectionism

Every day, we're bombarded with images and messages prescribing how we should look, work and act. Success stories saturate the internet and social media, without any mention of the frustration or years spent toiling away to reach that point. We are led to believe that perfection is attainable.

But there are crucial differences between striving for excellence and being shackled by the impossible goals of perfectionism. "When we think of a perfectionist, we think of someone who is lauded for their exemplary achievements. This is not the case," explains psychologist and author Dr. Tamar Chansky. "Perfectionism is a cognitive distortion—the idea that things can ever be perfect, which they cannot. Holding this mind-set doesn't lead to productivity or pride. Instead, it's correlated with depression."

The quest for perfection can act as a shield to protect against potential failure, suffering, rejection or disappointment. Yet paradoxically, it leads to a perpetual feeling of inadequacy. Fantasies of Doing Something Great can become so paralyzing that it's difficult to move beyond the first few hiccups or mistakes. Worries about making the right decision in a sea of endless possibilities can lead to continual switching, amounting to nothing. The stress and judgment that stems from perfectionism is exhausting and can negatively impact relationships, especially if you demand the same from friends and loved ones.

We can become so accustomed to the anxiety that comes with aiming for perfection that we stop noticing it, but it's never too late to counteract these tendencies. First, it's important to distinguish between excellence and perfection. And then we need to identify and label the unhealthy inner chatter as the catalyst of our perfectionism. Once that's done, we can generate more realistic and encouraging voices. Think about *why* you want to accomplish a goal, rather than focusing on the outcome.

Remember, everyone is imperfect. As British philosopher Alan Watts once suggested, you can think of yourself as a cloud. "Did you ever see a cloud that was misshapen? Or a badly designed wave? No, they always do the right thing," he said. "But if you would treat yourself for a while as a cloud or wave, you'll realize that you can't make a mistake whatever you do. Even if you do something that seems to be totally disastrous, it will all come out in the wash somehow or other."

SPACE BAKERY

by Molly Mandell

Bread may be a staple food here on Earth but can be a life-threatening hazard in space. "Crumbs are a huge issue," explains Sebastian Marcu, co-founder of Bake in Space—a German company aiming to make bread that can be consumed in the cosmos. "On Earth, crumbs will land in your toaster tray. But in microgravity, they fly around with no way to contain them." Midway into the flight of Gemini 3 in 1965, American astronaut John Young discovered the potential danger when he pulled out a corned beef sandwich that he had smuggled aboard (perhaps it had seemed more appealing than the rehydratable hot dogs and prepared food cubes that he had been sent to test). Young quickly realized that free-flying crumbs could land in astronauts' eyes or throats, or make their way into equipment. He never got to eat his sandwich. It was the first—and, until now, last—sandwich to enter space. Imitation sandwiches, with tortillas filling in for sliced bread, have meanwhile become popular alternatives. But imitations don't cut it in Germany, where there is a bakery on nearly every city corner and around 3,200 varieties of bread. "This is about much more than making a few astronauts happier," Marcu clarifies. "The project is a stepping stone for human exploration of space." Bake in Space aims to develop technology that makes the entire process possible aboard spacecraft, from growing grain to actually baking loaves of bread. "Eventually, we hope that space exploration will no longer be reliant on regular food deliveries from Earth." Crumbs aren't the only challenge for Bake in Space, however. If heat escapes from the oven, invisible bubbles of hot air can form and pose a risk to those on board. Baking and eating bread may be a tried and tested process on Earth, but whether it will become so simple in other parts of our galaxy is yet to be determined. *Photography by Aaron Tilley & Styling by Lucy-Ruth Hathaway*

ALEX ANDERSON

Homo Ludens

What is "at play" in our instinct to play?

Our taxonomic name, *homo sapiens*, identifies us as thinking beings. However, our distinctiveness does not lie exclusively in the mind—a point social scientists have often emphasized by offering new appellations for our species. Two of the more interesting of these, used by competing scholars during the mid-20th century, designate us as "makers"—*homo faber*—and as "players"—*homo ludens*. As makers, we labor to improve our environments, often ingeniously with tools. Our work defines us. As players, by contrast, we shape our existence in less utilitarian pursuits—leisure and recreation. So our play also defines us.

At first, homo ludens seems to be the more intriguing classification, but it may not really distinguish us. After all, hardly any other creature uses tools or makes things, but lots of animals play. Dogs chase their tails, fetch balls, catch Frisbees, chase one another. Cats pounce on fake mice and strike out at feet from under couches. Animal behaviorist Gordon Burghardt has found that monitor lizards play much like dogs, although in slow motion. He also surmises, on abundant evidence, that leaping fish often do so as a form of play.

How then, does play make homo sapiens distinctive? For most animals, play is almost exclusively a youthful activity. Fox and bear cubs are much more playful than adults. Their clumsy imitations of fighting or hunting seem almost purely for fun, but attentive mothers constrain their frolicking, which helps prepare them

for adulthood. Pet dogs, unlike foxes or bears, remain much more puppylike and playful as they age. Their domesticated lives of abundant food and low stress over millennia have emphasized juvenile their traits. This rare tendency, called "neoteny" by evolutionary biologists, is something they share, oddly enough, with their human caretakers.

Unlike other adult primates, our arms are short (like young chimps), and our maturation is long. According to Koen Tanghe, a philosopher at Ghent University, "we are designed by nature and evolution to continue playing throughout life." This playfulness helps us fill our leisure, but it also impacts virtually everything we do. As makers, it allows us to take joy in work, or to momentarily dispense with practicality, take risks, and find new ways of doing things. As thinkers, playfulness builds mental flexibility, foresight and empathy.

So, evolutionarily, playfulness seems to define us very broadly as homo ludens; it shapes our development, our work and our thinking. We also amuse ourselves differently than other creatures. Human play encompasses a huge range of activities and structures. Leaving aside art, music, theater, poetry and other cultural pursuits, leisure "play" can include the spontaneous, cublike amusement of toddlers, sedentary games of luck and calculation, contests of strength or endurance, and grand athletic spectacles enacted before crowds of thousands and viewing audiences of billions.

Sport, of all our forms of play, is the most complex and the most different from the amusements of animals. Sports involve complicated spatial limits defined by geometries of lines, arcs and circles inscribed on tracks or turf, and rules codified in staggeringly comprehensive catalogs (the official rule book for professional American football runs to 81 pages). Most casual participants in these games adhere to the constraints according to their abilities or the intensity of the competition. More committed athletes hone their skills with practice, and amplify their capabilities with specialized equipment—shoes, gloves, belts, bats, blades, clubs, sticks, poles. They group themselves with uniforms and mascots and pit themselves against similarly clad and represented rivals.

Professional competitors, battling under lights and cameras may not be having much fun, but they provide amusement to idle spectators watching from grandstands or through LED screens. As Tanghe explains, "our play instinct… is instrumental in the passive enjoyment of sports as it allows us to identify with an athlete or a team." Fans live the game, exult in victories as if they were their own, and drag losses dejectedly into work on Monday mornings.

As atavistic as these contests might seem, the spectacle of sport, so different from the play of animals and so typically human, helps justify our designation as homo ludens—but we may still want to dignify ourselves as "thinkers."

Photograph: Stephen Kugler

The wedding singer at whose wedding nobody sang.

JOHN CLIFFORD BURNS

Omar Souleyman

Omar Souleyman is a dabke musician from northeastern Syria, where, before exile, he was a prolific and popular wedding performer. In 2007, his music was repackaged and resold to the world via the American record label Sublime Frequencies. Since then, Souleyman has played Glastonbury, collaborated with Björk and ended up on stage at a Nobel Peace Prize concert. Much has been written about the black-swan quality of his career trajectory, how his music—so commonplace in the Levant—became "cult" for an audience outside of the context in which it was originally produced, and what that means for cultural colonialism. Souleyman will not entertain questions pertaining to his public image, but it's obvious that he exudes as much charisma as his music does danceability. Asked about his new album and daily life, Souleyman tells us that work is his priority, and that he yearns to return to Syria.

Your song "Warni Warni" was played at a wedding I recently attended. What makes your music so well-suited to such a specific occasion? It makes people dance. And that song is particularly beautiful because it talks about two people who are in love.

Who sang at your own wedding? Unfortunately, there was no music played at my wedding because someone in my family died around the same time. And, in Syria, whenever someone dies, either we postpone the wedding or we have a silent one. So, my own wedding was done without any sign of joy or celebration.

You have a large family. Are you easy to live with? I have six sons and three daughters and I'm very easy to live with! I can adapt pretty quickly.

What is one lesson you have instilled in each of your children? Respect is the most important lesson I've taught them—to respect those who are older and to maintain ethics wherever they go. They are all studying, and I always advise them to keep on doing it.

What's the first thing you do after waking up? I drink a cup of coffee and smoke a cigarette right after I go to the bathroom. I especially love Turkish coffee.

Do you consider anything to be missing from your life? I miss going back to my country. That's the only thing I need. Otherwise, I don't lack anything.

Photographs: Marsý Hild Þórsdóttir

Is there anything in your life that you feel you have too much of? No, nothing exaggerated. Just the things I need. My only hope is for the war to end in Syria so that I can go back and live with the people that I have always known and have always lived with. Life in Europe and the USA is pleasant, but a human being cannot really be at peace unless he is in his own country.

What causes you most stress? I'm not so easily stressed—it takes a lot. But if there's a problem hindering my work in any way, then I get really stressed because I believe that work is my priority in life. But I usually don't let it out on other people. I only stress out between me and myself.

What is the biggest influence on your work at present? The audience is always my biggest influence, or my biggest motivation. I have to face a new public every week. I have to be ready and I have to renew my style each time.

Sometimes, I get inspired by old tunes but I don't cover songs from other artists.

You often collaborate with other musicians. What's your favorite part of that process? I've always collaborated with other artists. Even when I was in Syria, I would consult poets about lyrics. Six or seven years ago, I recorded a song with Björk. She was the only person with whom I've worked very closely in the West. I visited her house.

"I miss going back to my country. That's the only thing I need. Otherwise, I don't lack anything."

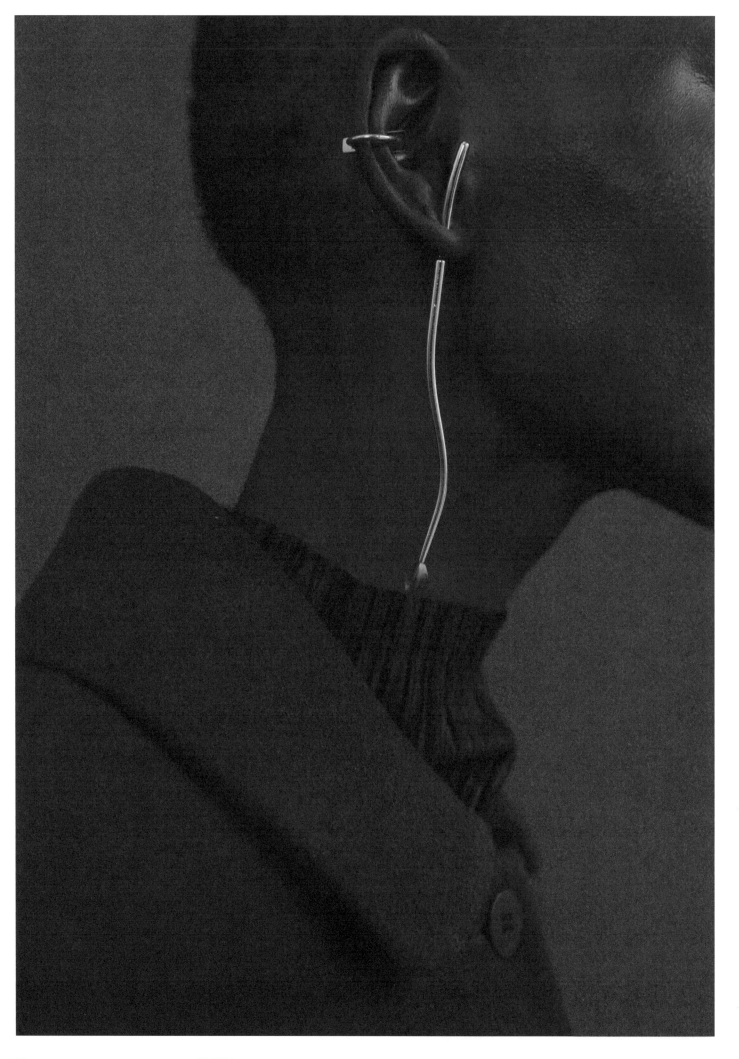

STARTERS

PIP USHER

On The Hook

Our love/hate relationship with songs that get stuck in our heads.

The word "earworm" is a direct translation of the German *ohrwurm*, which has been used in Germany since the late 1950s. Left: Earring by Paula Mendoza Jewelry.

Play Pharrell Williams' "Happy" and I bet an earworm wriggles its way into your brain. It'll start innocently enough, a few snippets of the international chart-topping and impossibly infectious track on loop. But later that day, you might find yourself humming it as you prepare dinner. Wake up the next morning and it may still be burrowed deep, the refrain sliding into your consciousness without warning.

Also known as involuntary musical imagery (INMI), the experience of spontaneously recalling a tune and then getting it stuck in your head on repeat is a common one. Its prevalence lies in the myriad ways that we can catch one. "The most frequent trigger is recent exposure to the actual song," says Dr. Kelly Jakubowski, a postdoctoral research assistant at Durham University's depart-

ment of music. "But we also often get songs in our heads that we haven't heard in months or years due to memory associations, such as seeing a word that reminds us of the song lyrics, or a picture or person that reminds us of the particular song."

According to Jakubowski, certain types of people are particularly prone to catching the musical bug. There are the music buffs who engage a lot with their passion, either by playing instruments or by spending their time at concerts. Unsurprisingly, this proximity means they tend to catch more earworms. But one's susceptibility can also be personality-based, with "people who score highly on the personality traits of 'openness to experience' and 'neuroticism,' and people who have more obsessive-compulsive traits" also experiencing earworms at a high-

er frequency. While they can be distracting, Jakubowski is quick to debunk any suggestion that this phenomenon is always annoying. "Research has consistently shown that around two-thirds of earworm experiences are rated as emotionally pleasant or neutral," she says. "When we do find an earworm annoying, this is often due to it being a song that we don't like or it causing distractions when we need our full attention on a task requiring auditory resources."

Popular songs are more likely to turn into earworms, as are newer releases. Tempo and melody count too: A song set at a faster speed with more generic melodic contours has a higher chance of getting stuck in our heads. In other words, we didn't stand a chance when it came to "Happy." You may as well follow Pharrell's advice and clap along.

A new word for a new era of known unknowns and unknown knowns.

TRISTAN RUTHERFORD

Word: Smupid

Etymology: Simply *smart + stupid = smupid*. *Meaning*: In their doomsayer of a book, *The Age of Earthquakes*, authors Douglas Coupland, Hans-Ulrich Obrist and Shumon Basar define *smupid* thusly: "The mental state where we acknowledge that we've never been smarter as individuals, and yet somehow we've never felt stupider."

For Coupland and pals, it's all the internet's fault. Those pesky computers are so clever that we can lodge our entire brains in their cloudlike embrace, and never have to remember a single thing. Apart from our password. Or our mother's maiden name if we forget that.

Except that the ability to upload our memories, then re-download them as necessary, has created a wireless impotence. And confusion and technophobia in equal measure.

The feeling of utter stupidly in an age of unlimited possibility is a novel concept. We have access to 30 million songs on Spotify, but can't wire the plug to the Sonos without looking on YouTube. Because that is information we don't have to store on our own "hard drive"— clever but dumb at the same time. The trauma of digital vertigo is another challenge in the epoch of smupid. The World Wide Web gives you a greater knowledge base than Albert Einstein, but makes you more impatient. Think about making vacation plans through a travel agent. According to *The Age of Earthquakes*, that's "a slower process invented in times of less technology." It's unlikely we'll step inside a travel agency when booking a week in Barcelona. Instead, our ability to cross-reference 150 airlines in a nanosecond, while making a cup of tea, is astounding. But the cacophony of flight times and car rental options makes us fretful. As does choosing one of the city's 17,000 Airbnb apartments. After three hours of online anxiety, a vacation is needed to recover from the act of booking one.

As Coupland, Obrist and Basar attest: "The future is even smupider." That's if we don't stop Dropboxing our DNA on a minute-by-minute basis. Stepping into the travel agency for 30 minutes may actually be quicker than scouring Booking.com. Downgrading to a dumbphone might make you more productive. And reading an Agatha Christie novel might still your senses more than a fruitless trawl through Netflix.

Photograph: Aaron Tilley, Set Design: Sandy Suffield

CRUNCHING NUMBERS

by Molly Mandell

From the abacus to the iPhone app, calculation tools have existed for thousands of years. The first electronic calculator was invented in 1961 and was roughly the size of a typewriter. Requiring an electrical outlet, it could rival the cost of a new car. The first handheld calculator became commercially available in 1970, causing a seismic shift in the world's way of doing arithmetic. Though pocket calculators have become increasingly obsolete since the late '90s, when cell phones with calculator applications hit the market, they have yet to disappear. For some, the satisfaction of pressing buttons outweighs the calculator's monofunctionality. *Braun's BNE001 Calculator (top), designed by Dieter Rams, and MUJI's 8 Digit Desk Calculator (bottom) make for great workspace companions, while Casio's Calculator Watch (middle) can solve equations on the go.*

ELLIE VIOLET BRAMLEY

Beyond Reasonable Doubt

Why being good at your job can leave you feeling like a fraud, and how to overcome it.

What do Maya Angelou, Neil Gaiman and Zadie Smith have in common? Aside from being three of the greatest writers of our time, they have all struggled with imposter phenomenon—the feeling that one is out of place, underqualified, not intelligent or creative enough or just generally lacking. It's the sinking sense that one's successes are merely a matter of timing, luck, the kindness of others—never one's own talent or skill.

Even 11 books in, Angelou worried she would be found out—resonating with the words of philosopher Bertrand Russell: "The stupid are cocksure while the intelligent are full of doubt." Ironically, the specter of impostor phenomenon often looms the largest at precisely the time we are doing our best work. But this self-doubt can also silence us at moments when we might otherwise move forward.

Coined in 1978 by two American psychologists, Pauline Clance and Suzanne Imes, it is a phenomenon that has tangled roots, different for each sufferer. Known to afflict more women than men, and to be more common among minorities, it is a frequent complaint of those who grew up in families that placed emphasis on achievement. It is also a curse of perfectionists, for whom the slightest flaw becomes synonymous with failure.

Author Valerie Young has spent the last 20 years helping people avoid feeling phony. Her advice for sufferers: "If you want to stop feeling like an impostor, you have to stop thinking like one."

The first step, she explains, is to normalize the feelings. After all, "The most talented and accomplished people have deep moments of self-doubt." And then reframe them: "Step back. If I could call in an actor to play the part of me who didn't feel like an impostor, how would I think about this exact same situation."

Next comes perseverance: "Keep going regardless of how you feel. People often wait until they feel more confident to write their book or try to get their art into a gallery." But that's not how it works. "You have to do the thing that's scary, accept the fact that it's not going to be perfect. Over time, you will start to feel more confident."

If all that feels like a lifetime's work, then take comfort during your next moment of self-doubt—at least you're in good company.

Rebel without a pause: A firebrand photographer
and visual activist reflects on a decade's work.

JESSICA LYNNE

Zanele Muholi

Vile, Gothenburg, Sweden, 2016.
Gelatin silver print. The photograph
opposite forms part of Muholi's ongoing
self-portrait series titled *Somnyama
Ngonyama (Hail, the Dark Lioness).*

Zanele Muholi approaches the craft of photography with a fervent political mission. As an educator, she is relentlessly dedicated to mentoring and empowering a new generation of storytellers. Throughout the past decade, the South African photographer has created a tender and intimate archive of portraits of black lesbian and transgender communities living in South Africa for her critically acclaimed series *Faces and Phases*. For her most recent body of work, *Somnyama Ngonyama (Hail, the Dark Lioness)*, Muholi places herself in front of the camera in a self-portraiture series that responds to the entanglement of injustice and blackness. Above all, Muholi's images challenge us to renegotiate the very act of looking and to consider its potential as a radical act.

You describe yourself as a visual activist. What exactly does that mean, and why is it important to use that language as an identification marker? Identifying as a visual activist specifically refers to the use of photography as a political tool. It refers to the development of visual materials that speak to the state of emergency in South Africa in the post-apartheid era. It addresses the ongoing violations of human rights in spaces where such violations are not supposed to happen, yet need to be documented. Take, for instance, the ongoing racial attacks that are happening in America. To be a visual activist means that you rely on a sense of community journalism to document realities without expecting mainstream media to do so on your behalf. For example, there have been a number of hate crimes in South Africa. Most of them transformed our neighborhoods into crime scenes full of brutalized black bodies. We have a responsibility to document that. We can't just fold our arms. I personally believe in media, and though the mainstream sometimes distorts information, I have a responsibility to revise that visual history alongside my colleagues in a manner that makes sense to those who are living that reality.

I'm particularly interested in the way you have traversed the boundaries of portraiture, such as with *Faces and Phases*, and self-portraiture, with *Somnyama Ngonyama (Hail, the Dark Lioness)*. Can you talk about the nuances that exist between these two approaches to image making? On a basic level, *Faces and Phases* features lesbian-identifying folks and trans folks. In this project, the participants are photographed in ways in which they are most comfortable showing up in the world. *Somnyama Ngonyama* makes use of historical events and media reports that people might be aware of. This project speaks to the ongoing consequences of racism as well as the need for complex self-representation. For this project, I tried to capture myself as I have moved along in different places as a black woman, as a member of the LGBTQI community. But, whether in front of the camera or not, in both projects what is there is a commitment to telling the truth about my communities.

What has surprised you most about the act of self-portraiture? What have you learned about yourself? The biggest lessons have not been connected to the technical aspects of photography. Rather, slowly but surely, I'm learning how to rest. I have come back to my home of Durban and for the first time in my life, I just need an absolute pause. So, more than anything, the lesson has to do with self-love and self-respect. This reminds me of the Audre Lorde quote in which she states that "caring for myself is not self-indulgence, it is self-preservation, and that is an act of political warfare." Preservation is its own form of resistance. And at a certain point, your body will not allow you to keep moving at the same pace despite your good intentions. As much as my activism means to me, I'm reminded that I have to take care of myself.

If someone were to stumble upon your work in the future, how would you like for it to be received? I have learned that my photographs occupy a political space, and because of that, I would want people to remember that a person like me once existed. That it is possible for others to write or rewrite their histories, their black histories, their queer histories, their trans histories into existence. When I enter into a space, I'm doing it for the next generation in my communities who are seeking role models. I want to be remembered as someone who is using visual culture and visual activism to articulate the vastness of our presence.

Photograph: © Zanele Muholi, courtesy of the artist, Stevenson, Cape Town / Johannesburg, and Yancey Richardson, New York

Daniela Soto-Innes

Ambition has taken her career from cleaning lettuce to serving award-winning Mexican food to President Barack Obama.

In 2014, chefs Daniela Soto-Innes and Enrique Olvera opened Cosme—an acclaimed restaurant in New York City inspired by their native Mexico. Only nine years earlier, Soto-Innes started her first professional job in the food industry: cleaning lettuce and cutting strawberry tops at a Marriott hotel outside of Houston. Now a James Beard award winner, she maintains the tenacious attitude that propelled her to this point, accompanied by equal doses of playfulness and warmth. It's a necessary balance for a healthy kitchen, she says, while reminiscing about early food memories and explaining how creating a menu is a bit like a romantic date.

What are some of your strongest food-related memories? Mexican cinnamon and toasted corn—that's my childhood. Everyone in Mexico relates to that. We all have that sense of smell and taste connected to memory—those moments when you just want to close your eyes and stay there. I also think of my great-grandmother, grandmother and mother—all women who love to cook. My great-grandmother, from Mexico, went to school for cooking in Paris and across Europe; she was an incredible cook, and I was lucky enough to meet her. My grandmother managed a bakery in Mexico—I would steal bread from there all the time, even though I couldn't see above the tables. And my mother's dream was to become a chef but her parents said that it wasn't a real job, so she became a lawyer. She took me to her cooking classes though, so it was normal for me. I'm 27, but I feel so old because I've been cooking in kitchens for as long as I can remember—from 14 until now, with only one real vacation in between.

What does childhood mean to you? Pure happiness with no baggage. When you're a child, you don't think of the problems or negativity around you. You don't even think that things are necessarily positive. You just keep asking why and exploring. You're constantly amazed. If we could just stay that way, staying conscious of what's around us, everyone would be so much happier.

Do you hope to instill that child-like attitude in the diner? When you expect too much of one thing, you get disappointed. Cosme might be a destination place, but we want that destination to be a happy one. Everything here has very simple, clean lines. Our plates are all white because it's easier; I wear all black because it's easier to get dressed in the morning. We don't need crazy, fancy things if we're using the best products available. We want people to know that we're just trying to be us and nothing else. We leave pretentiousness aside. A lot of cooks here, myself included, have worked at "fine dining" restaurants but, for us, Cosme is much more about who we have around us, their stories, and the hope that we can introduce those stories to others. We're always cooking and dancing! When there's serious work, of course, we're serious. But this is a beautiful playground in which we admire, learn and worry about each other, and we want to do the same for the people who come here.

So, happy chefs make better food? Cooking is like a dance: You need the right coordination. I don't hire cooks—I hire personalities. If you're nice to me or to other people, I will hire you and teach you how to cook. Sometimes it bites me in the ass and is more difficult, and people take issue, but I say, "Just give it some time." And now some of those very people are among the best here. If you have a willingness to work and understand that problems are just frustrations in your head, then you'll be able to do anything.

That resonates with how you started your career, just pushing yourself into kitchens. I was just there. I'm a very hyper person, but I'm quieter when I'm cooking. It's like therapy. I love yoga, but cooking gives me discipline. You have to pay attention, you have to listen, you have to taste—you have to use all of your senses. When I'm not in a good mood, I won't cook.

I've heard that you speak mostly Spanish in your kitchen, despite a very diverse staff. When the whole staff is native Spanish speakers, I like to switch it to English, and then the inverse for those who don't speak Spanish as their first language. We mix and match.

Cosme's menu has numerous untranslated terms. Was that a conscious decision? Some things are so native to Mexico that you shouldn't touch them. Like, how do you translate *tamal*? Or *conchas*? Do you call it "brioche"? It sounds pretentious if you translate it. Of course, we're not going to say *queso* for cheese, but we like not to touch things that are authentic.

Are you trying to educate diners at the same time? I think you need to provide something that people will be interested in. If you're familiar with part of a conversation, then you'll stay a little bit longer. It's like a date: When your date says something that you like, you think, "Okay, I'll stay a few more minutes." A menu is a conversation between you and the diner. Maybe they'll recognize one thing or nothing at all, but when they eat it, other familiarities might arise. I moved from Mexico to Texas when I was 12, and I feel I can better understand other cultures because of that. In Texas, there were so many different people—as in New York—and that influences my cooking. I like to incorporate techniques that look similar. *Mole*, for example, is very similar to curry.

Who inspires you in the food world? People who are nice to their staff have the best kitchens. Chefs who are egotistical forget about cooking. I never want to forget how to treat people right. You also need to know who you are outside of the kitchen. Most of the restaurant world has no mindfulness, only effort. Mindfulness goes along with caring, and effort goes along with burning out. We need to be on equal terms with both.

Tina Frey Designs

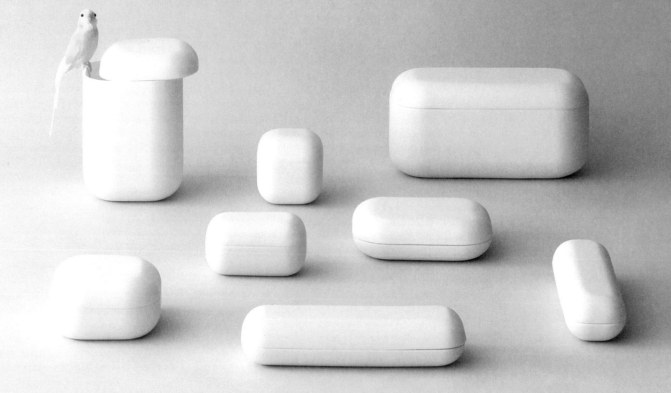

2
Features

Kilo

Inside the immersive world of *Lakisha Kimberly Robinson*. Words by *Sala Elise Patterson*.

Kish

Photography by *Katie McCurdy* & Styling by *Sue Choi*

"Someone else's label on me is not really my narrative." Kilo Kish is talking about being a black woman in the music industry but could just as easily be discussing her music, or any of her other creative pursuits. The 27-year-old singer-songwriter, model, designer and artist is as allergic to categorization as she is to predictability.

In her relatively short career, Kish (née Lakisha Kimberly Robinson) has already put out an LP (*Reflections In Real Time*, 2016) and three EPs (*Homeschool*, 2012; *Across*, 2014; *Across Remixes*, 2015); modeled for *Lucky*, *Vice* and *Vogue*; collaborated with Childish Gambino and The Internet; produced two capsule fashion collections; launched her lifestyle label, KSA; and curated *Real—Safe*, a performance and exhibition that debuted in July at HVW8 Gallery in Los Angeles.

According to Kish, boredom is to blame for her hyperproductivity and eclectic interests. After studying design at the Fashion Institute of Technology and visual art at the Pratt Institute in New York, Kish came to music through an accident that has passed into urban lore: After a few beers one night, she jokingly freestyled over a beat, and her roommate, rapper Smash Simmons, captured it in the home studio. The recording circulated and listeners fell hard for her buoyant, half-sung/half-spoken lyrical style. Underground buzz led to mainstream press. A rising star was born.

Today, Kish hits pause for our interview from her home in Los Angeles. Her conversation is a lot like her lyrics: thoughtful, real. Not surprisingly, she thinks in terms of projects and discoveries, not trajectory and career. While some young artists might be paralyzed by the big question marks—what's next and when, and what could it look like—Kish seems to thrive on them.

Your music has been referred to as rap, post-rap, art pop, experimental hip-hop, psychedelic pop, neo-psychedelia and new wave. How would *you* describe your music? When people ask, I usually say pop, because people shut up at pop. You're not being pretentious, saying, "Oh, it's experimental." No, it's not anything cool, it's just pop and I don't want to talk about it anymore! Actually, I

Previous spread: Kish wears a top by BreeLayne and earrings by FARIS. Opposite: She wears a coat by BreeLayne, top and shoes by Topshop, trousers by bassike and earrings by FARIS.

"I see my music as conversational. The songwriting is very stream of consciousness."

Set design: Samantha McCurdy

"Music requires more freedom than design. It can't be perfect; some nuance is nice."

FEATURES

see all music as pop, just a capsule of time from different artists. To me, genres have become fragmented. I'm thinking, "Why would you want to box yourself in?" I can understand if you are coming out of a scene and you've named it yourself and you're making work together. In that way, maybe I could see putting a label on it.

When do you feel like you turned a corner with your music and went from playing around to seeing yourself as a musician? I keep thinking, "Okay, now I'm a real artist." But then I think, "Nope, I'm still not." But I would say that *Reflections* feels a lot different to me than the other music. It was much more personal. On the EP I put out before that, I was slowly dipping my toe into the idea, but with *Reflections* I got to a level where the music was totally mine. I was hitting a place where it felt right, fully me. Now I'm trying to use what I've learned about music to create spaces, feelings and complete worlds. I'm trying to capture what is. What does it feel like standing

down, coming up with musical phrases rather than just ideas. Eventually, I collect everything and figure out how to put it together. That's where I am with my next album. Taking a year's worth of notes and trying to figure out what I want to do.

I see my music as conversational. The songwriting is very stream of consciousness. I take cues from film and try to create a world around each song. And I try to make it as dramatic as possible. I see myself primarily as a designer because that's the approach that I take to most things I do. I try to design an experience more than anything else—with an art show or even my album or music. It's all placed in a way that is intentional.

Does your creative process translate easily from one discipline to the other? Does one inform the other? Not really. For example, now that I'm learning instruments and have more of a hand in producing my music, I realize music requires more freedom than design. It can't be perfect; some nuance is nice. You have to

"*I keep thinking, 'Okay, now I'm a real artist.' But then I think, 'Nope, I'm still not.'*"

at the ocean? Or what is it like to watch something physically grow? How do I capture what it actually is to be alive? Those are some of the concepts I'm working through now—things that are much more natural. I'm trying to remove as much of myself as possible because I don't want to make a second album about me.

What was your path to music from design? I got into music when I was about 20 years old. It was something I didn't know I knew how to do. But when my college financial aid lapsed for a year, I wasn't able to draw and paint [Kish was a fine arts major at Pratt before transferring to FIT]. But I was able to express myself in a different way, through music. I don't think that would have come about had I stayed in art class for four years.

Can you talk about your creative process? I come up with general ideas and then funnel them to whatever medium makes the most sense. Music is a weird one, though, because I'm always writing stuff

let it breathe. In design, I'm always thinking about what is modern— clean, clear, white, pristine. I'm very detail oriented. But in music, I'm learning to let go of the reins a bit more.

What I want to do with fashion and what I want to do musically don't inform each other, because musically I'm always focusing on more, more, more. How can I make it as bold and innovative as possible? As far as style, it's much more minimal and pulled back. For example, I wear the same thing every day: jeans and a T-shirt.

To the extent that you ever have a typical day, what does it look like? Super regimented and I don't really see anyone for the majority of it. Typically, I'll wake up around six and walk a mile to get a juice and avocados with my boyfriend. Then I will pray, meditate, stretch. I have a lot of excess energy, so if I don't do that kind of stuff then I get very antsy. I have an overactive kind of brain. After that I study French—I've been practicing every day for four

Previous spread: Kish wears a top by Pari Desai, trousers by BreeLayne, a dress by bassike and earrings by FARIS. Opposite: She wears a coat by BreeLayne, top by Topshop, trousers by bassike and earrings by FARIS.

months—because I don't like to jump into working immediately. I am also learning guitar, so I practice that, then write for about an hour and read for another hour. Then, if I come up with an idea, I'll just work on it and take it as far as I can before it requires input from other people.

In fact, a lot of your work is collaborative. Is working with other people something you enjoy? I do and I don't. I love when people have their own unique skill set that can enhance my work and bring it to the next level. That's what my boyfriend [Ray Brady] does. He's my producer and understands me well enough that I can pass the baton on and he can carry it and make the song better. I also collaborate frequently with Sam Massey on video and photography, and with Emmanuel Olunkwa, a photographer.

It's hard because I have such a doctrine about my work, and when so many hands touch it, the essence of the work starts to not really be yours anymore. With too many chefs in the kitchen, you just end up with something trendy. That's because in 2017, we all have such a large reference bank of information. Even if you didn't want to see something, you cannot unsee it. It is still cataloged in your brain and it is going to affect it. Even if you don't think it will. That's why I prefer one-on-one collaborations, and I try to make sure both parties are going in the same direction, or that the directions complement each other.

What's the concept behind *Real —Safe*? The concept branched out of *Reflections*. It's about humans, our interactions with each other in a visual era and the way we behave, and what role technology plays in us becoming closer or more distant.

The show was a performance installation. I hired a bunch of actors to pretend to be gallery patrons. The public enters the room one at a time and assumes that everyone is just there at the party like them. Then, on a musical cue, the actors stop and stare at the person. And they do that for 10 to 20 seconds. Then the person walks through and there are some films and a recorded version [of the space] so they can watch themselves. It was all a nod to social media and the way that we can exploit ourselves through social media. But

Kish released her debut studio album *Reflections in Real Time* on her own imprint label in 2016. It follows three EPs and a mixtape, and is intended to be a time capsule of her early twenties.

Above: Kish wears a coat by BreeLayne. Opposite: She wears a top and trousers by Shaina Mote, shoes by Topshop and earrings by FARIS.

when the person exploiting you shifts to somebody else, it doesn't feel the same. With social media, we can take pictures of ourselves and look for likes and actually be gratified by having eyes on us. But when eyes in real life are on us, it is a different experience. I was trying to shift the gaze a bit and ask the question, Why is attention so vital online and not in person? And what makes it different?

Social media is a constant theme in your work. You also seem to grapple with it. You shut down your Instagram account in 2016 and rebooted it, for example. Do you even like it? I do like it. I find it more interesting than anything else. I like the difference in behavior that you get out of people. Even just a comment section on You-Tube with people saying things they would never say in person. Where is the start of the line between how you are online and who you are in person? Some people would say that it doesn't really matter, but for me it's an interesting point to work with.

When do you expect your next album to come out? Sometime before fall 2018. But honestly, I don't know. I'm just starting the album now and I'm open to different processes. If we record the whole thing in three weeks, then great. If it takes another year and a half, then that's that. I'm open to whatever, as long as it comes out and feels good, like something I want it to be.

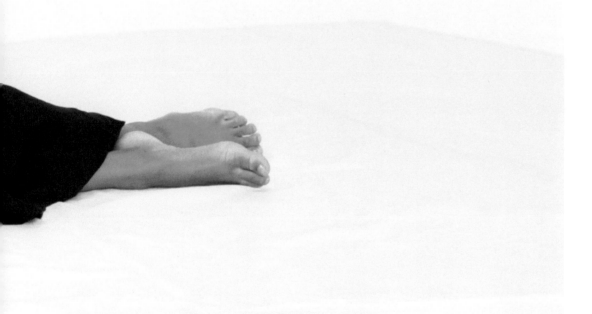

Kish wears a dress by bassike and earrings by FARIS.

Get in

Smile. Swim. Dazzle: Water ballet in the Hollywood hills.

Formation

Photography by Emma Hartvig

Emma Hartvig's series *The Swimmers* is the result of a meeting between the photographer and The Aqualillies—a water ballet troupe—earlier this year in Hollywood.

Though inspired by Esther Williams and the glamour of Los Angeles pool culture, Hartvig says her overall aim with the series was "to show how serious, hardworking and strong these swimmers are."

"Their bodies are engrossed and strengthened, heavier and lighter at the same time," says Hartvig. "I love the 'behind-the-scenes' of that whole world."

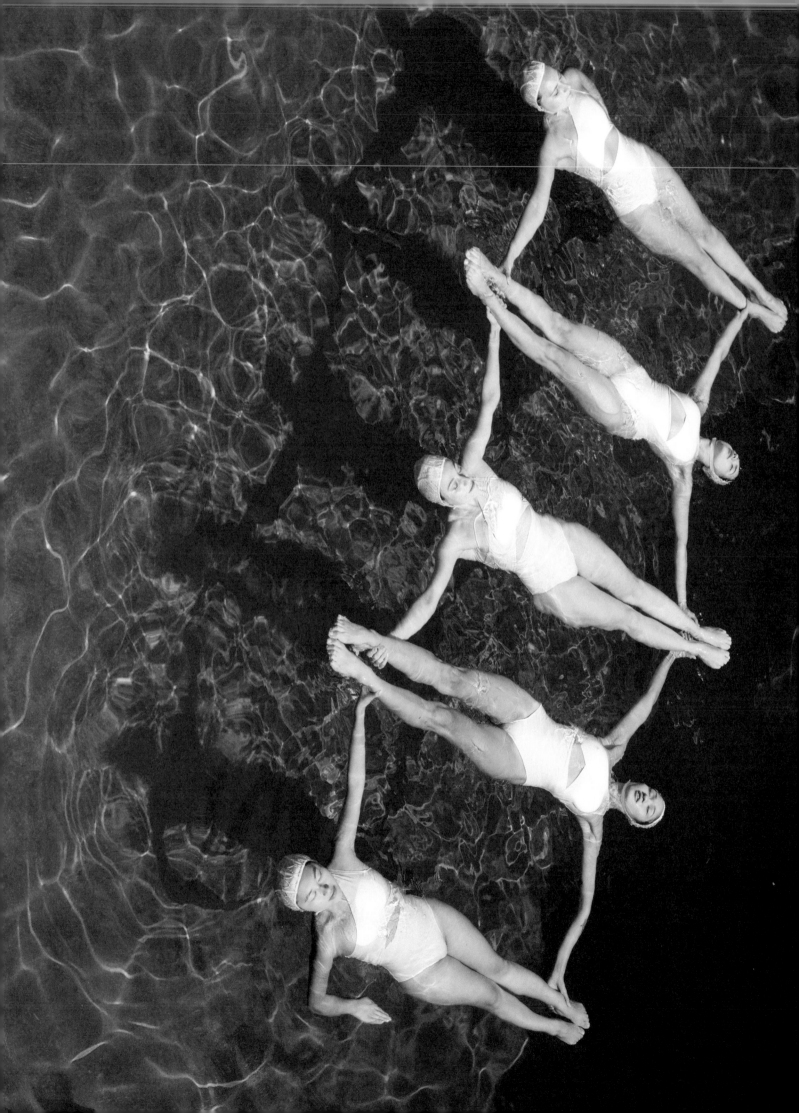

Exposure: Gordon Parks

Gordon Parks documented America: its violence, its beauty, its pride and its prejudice. During the mid-20th century, his fashion photography and celebrity commissions were tempered with reportage that exposed the nation to its injustices. Many of the themes that concerned him—racism, marginalization, poverty—remain as charged and complex today as they did then. Words by *Sala Elise Patterson* & Photography by *Gordon Parks*

Some artists create with a sense of purpose that extends beyond making something beautiful. American photographer Gordon Parks is a consummate example. Over a nearly seven-decade career, he used his camera to document "all the things I dislike about America—poverty, racism, discrimination." And he was consistent: consistently prolific, inspired and committed to fighting inequality. According to his daughter Leslie Parks, "He always wanted to show injustice. That's all he knew, so that's what he took photographs of."

Most people know Parks for his firsts: first African-American man to work at *Life* magazine, first to write and direct a Hollywood film (*The Learning Tree* in 1969)—or for a single iconic photograph or film. Few are aware of the breadth of his creativity, that he was also a self-taught pianist, composer and author of memoirs, poetry, novels and plays. Fewer still appreciate how he brought to the American mainstream the truth—ugly and beautiful—of people rendered invisible because of an unprivileged station in life. A child of those hidden truths, Parks compelled a reluctant America to account for them through images that mesmerized and seemed to ask: "Now that you've seen me, what are you going to do about it?"

Gordon Parks was born into a poor farming family in rural Kansas, the youngest of 15. His childhood was shaped as much by the stunning natural landscape as it was by the fear, hatred and violence he experienced as a young black man. Despite the hardships of living in segregated America, Parks' mother had great plans for him, placing "love, dignity and hard work over hatred," as he described in his autobiography, *A Choice of Weapons*. A young Parks responded by approaching life with ambition and purpose. Following his mother's instructions from her deathbed, at 16 he went to live with a sister in St. Paul, Minnesota. "[Go know] another kind of world, one with more hope and promising things," she implored. With the prairies of Kansas in his mind and her words in his ears, he set out.

That love, expectation and a religious upbringing served as a moral compass for Parks in the precarious years right after he left home. These values also eventually defined him as an artist. Even though he began his career as a fashion and portrait photographer, and later shot for major glossies, he never stopped pointing his camera at what was wrong in the world. "He did them concurrently," explains Amanda Smith, assistant director at The Gordon Parks Foundation. She

"Parks was consistent: consistently prolific, inspired and committed to fighting inequality."

Previous spread: Gordon Parks, *Evening Wraps at Dawn*, New York, New York, 1956.
Left: *Untitled*, ca. 1948 (one of Parks' many self portraits). Above: *Department Store*, Mobile, Alabama, 1956.

points to two stories Parks shot in 1956: one of a family living in Alabama under Jim Crow segregation, and another, a lush fashion feature. "It's amazing that the same photographer was able to use his camera so effectively for such different things."

This agility is especially remarkable given that Parks was self-taught. That is not to say he didn't study or approach his work with rigor. Rather, he educated himself into a skilled practitioner, reading "every book on art and photography I could afford." It is difficult to appreciate what it meant for a black man to break color barriers in 1950s America without the benefit of formal education. It is evidence of his determination, ingenuity and the staying power of his mother's words.

Parks' road to photography was circuitous. After leaving home as a teenager, he spent a long decade eking out a living at largely ungratifying jobs. But while working as a waiter on a railroad dining car at the age of 25, he thumbed through a magazine left by a co-worker. "There was a portfolio of photographs in it that I couldn't forget; they were of migrant workers. Dispossessed, beaten by dust, storms and floods... scrounging for work," he wrote. Parks was as mesmerized by what the images documented as by what they communicated—the depth of the subjects' humanity and their misery. He had never experienced so much in individual photographs.

For months, Parks studied the pictures and the names of the photographers who took them: Russell Lee, Walker Evans, Dorothea Lange and others. They were working for the Farm Security Administration on an initiative that photographed the lives of poor American farmers to "introduce America to Americans," as program director Roy Stryker would say. Little did Parks know that within seven years he would join them at the FSA and lay the

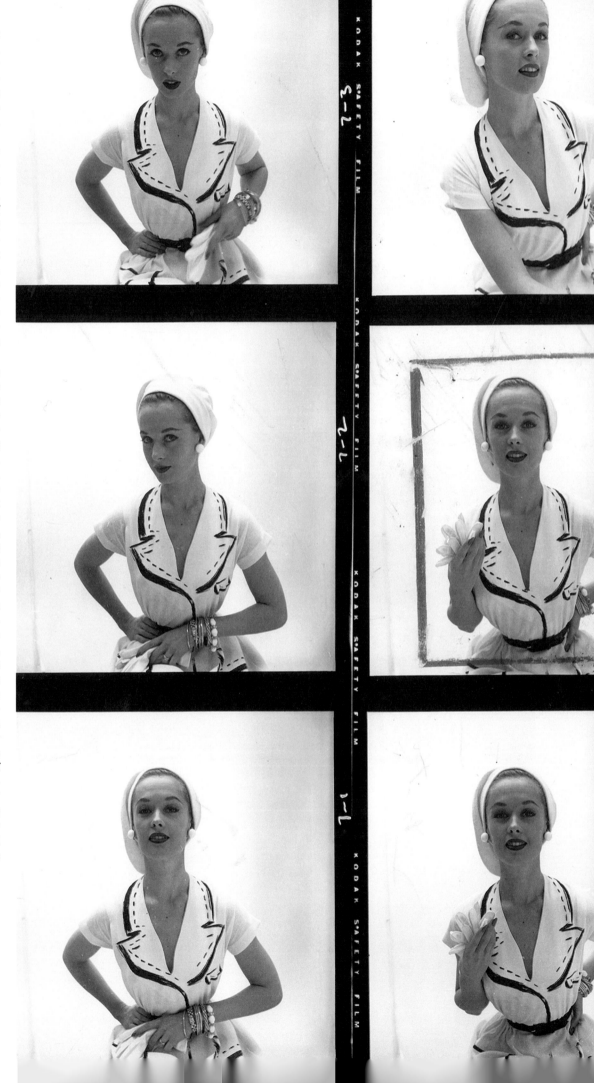

Untitled, New York, New York, 1952 offers a behind-the-scenes look at some of Gordon Parks' fashion commissions in the 1950s.

foundation for a remarkable career as a documentary photographer.

Ultimately Parks committed to photography because he realized its power to raise the social consciousness of the viewer, even—perhaps, especially—those who saw the world as flawless and fair. After months studying that FSA photo essay, he entered a pawnshop in Seattle and purchased his first camera (a Voigtländer Brillant), some film and a handbook on exposure. Parks started shooting: fashion and portraits and then a series on Chicago's impoverished South Side. Those early efforts won him his first big break in 1942—the prized Julius Rosenwald Fellowship and an invitation from Stryker to train with his idols at the FSA.

While at the FSA, Parks gained "discipline and a sense of direction." It is where he took one of his most celebrated photographs, *American Gothic* (1942), which played in image and title on American painter Grant Wood's 1930 painting of the same name. He shot Ella Watson, a black woman who cleaned the FSA offices, broom in hand, mop and American flag in the backdrop. That image came to symbolize the thrust of the then nascent civil rights movement—confronting America's broken promise to its black population.

Parks and his FSA colleagues fed the American imagination with images of African-American life that sharply contrasted with negative stereotypes prevalent at the time. When the FSA closed in 1943, Parks moved briefly to the Office of War Information where he photographed the Tuskegee Airmen, the first African-American military pilots in the US armed forces.

That period was followed by several years as a freelance fashion photographer, most notably for *Vogue*. There, he showcased a signature aesthetic, which photo historian and Gordon Parks Foundation board member Deborah Willis calls street style. "He situated models in haute couture dresses and stylized suits within the lively city. Readers could imagine themselves in the clothing, either waiting for a bus on Fifth Avenue or experiencing a flat tire on the way to a ball." She adds, "Gordon understood the importance of beauty in everyday life. He recognized desire and found a way to express it in many forms."

In 1948, Parks received the offer of a lifetime: to join *Life* magazine as a staff photographer. It was at *Life* that he cemented his reputation as an extraordinary photojournalist. He shot luminaries (Alexander Calder, Alberto Giacometti, Leonard Bernstein, Ralph Ellison, Muhammad Ali, Ingrid Bergman), religious and social movements (Black Panthers, the civil rights movement, Benedictine monks), fashion and reportage. But perhaps his greatest contribution to the national consciousness was exposing everyday moments in the lives of ordinary black and poor people in rural and urban America.

At *Life*, Parks became known as a champion of social causes and an authentic public photographic voice about blackness and deprivation. Aaron Bryant, curator of photography at the Smithsonian National Museum of African American History and Culture says Parks was about more than just civil rights. He was about human rights, using photography to comment on many kinds of discrimination—gender, class, socioeconomic, race, as well as regional. "He makes incredibly clear distinctions between the kinds of oppression that one can be subjugated to, and he can do it all in one photograph or series of photographs," Bryant explains.

Parks' sensitivity and compassion for his subjects allowed them to reveal their most honest selves. "He was always able to make his subjects feel comfortable. He was very charming," Leslie Parks says. Whether shooting Red Jackson, a young gang leader in Harlem; Flavio, a sickly boy living in a favela in Rio de Janeiro; the Fontenelle family, fraying at the seams in Harlem; or segregation

> "Parks committed to photography because he realized its power to raise the social consciousness of the viewer, even—perhaps, especially—those who saw the world as flawless and fair."

Opposite: *Untitled*, Watts, California, 1967, is one of many photographs Gordon Parks shot at civil rights rallies around the USA.

Below: *Untitled*, Shady Grove, Alabama, 1956, is one of the scenes of Americana for which Parks is celebrated.
Opposite: *Walburga, Baroness von Friesen*, Estoril, Portugal, 1951.

FEATURES

in the South, his photos captured the intimate consequences of societal dysfunction. That was critical in 1960s America, Bryant explains, when mainstream media propagated ideals of a universally accessible middle class. "Parks becomes the photographer that defines a genre that interrogates this other America and the myth of the American dream," he says.

Parks would stay at *Life* for more than two decades. The impact of that period on his legacy cannot be overstated. He worked for the magazine during its most influential years, which meant his photographs had a large American audience. For many, his stories offered a first-ever look at how stifled fellow Americans were by racial segregation, violence and poverty.

And Parks was shooting at *Life* before the era of Photoshop, as photographer Wing Young Huie writes in the foreword to Parks' autobiography, when "photographs were embedded with notions of truth." That extends equally to the suffering displayed and to the dignity of his subjects. Thus, *Life* readers took Parks' images at face value, as indisputable, even if they did not connect the human condition on display with the political landscape that made it possible. At its most effective, that kind of photography makes empathy possible and intervention feel necessary. On June 27, 2017, American rap phenomenon Kendrick Lamar released the music video for his song "Element." Poignant and cinematically relentless, it recreates four classic Parks images at key moments. Lamar and his co-directors (photographer Jonas Lindstroem and manager Dave Free) have created a respectful video befitting a musician who, according to *Rolling Stone*, raps with "cinematic precision" and "talks in colors."

There is a greater message in the gesture, however. As an artist whose music and videos tell stories that are essentially a call to action, Lamar is aligning himself with Parks around a common, aesthetically driven breed of activism. Although very different, both men speak harsh truths about America, many of them the same, even at a distance of decades.

The reality is, America has never fully acknowledged or reconciled the racial injustices Parks captured with his camera. And, it makes efforts to do so only when forced by catastrophic events—Charlottesville, Flint, Charleston, Sanford. Perhaps Parks' legacy, then, is to show us how beauty can create a narrative where words won't. Leslie Parks offers: "Let's not forget what he taught us with his photographs, what he wrote about, the lessons. It's nice to go back and look at his work—and never forget."

"America has never fully reconciled the racial injustices Parks captured with his camera."

Untitled, Miami, Florida, 1970, part of a series Gordon Parks shot of Muhammad Ali in the '60s and early '70s.

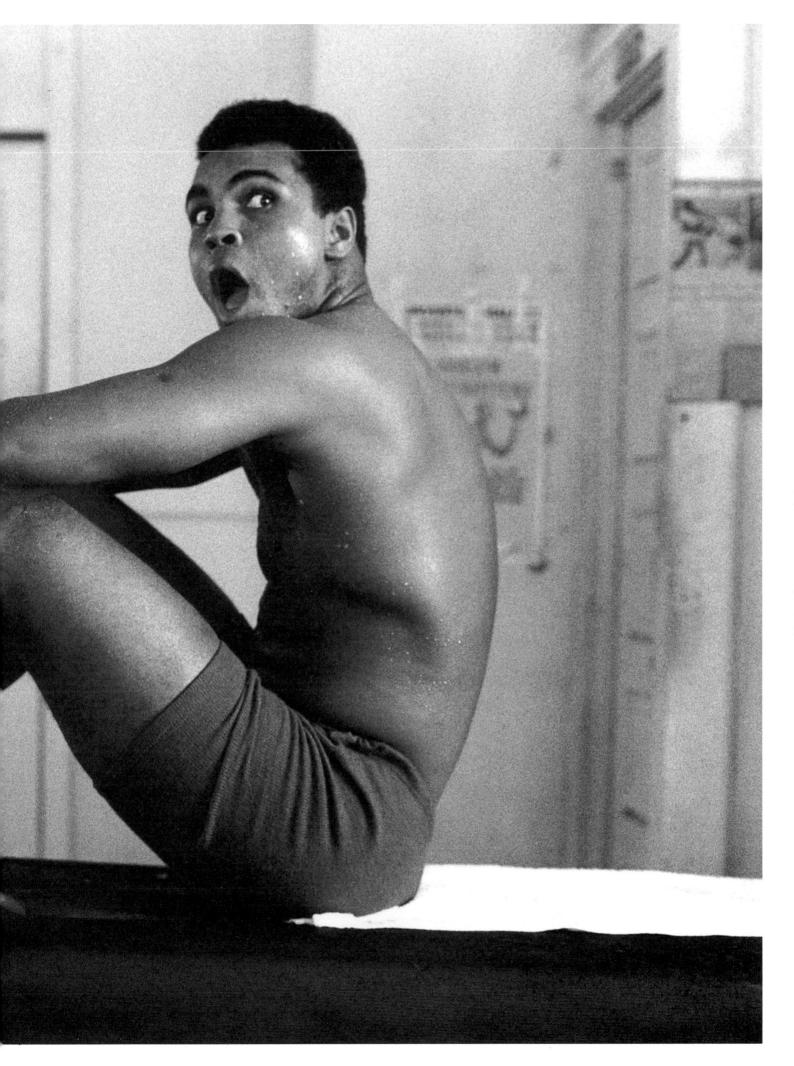

The sonatas and fantasies of a piano can stir our most grandiose and ghostly emotions.

Piani

The st

Photography by *Mark Sanders* & Styling by *David Lamb*

Opposite: Olivier wears a suit by Canali and a collarless shirt by Margaret Howell.

Above: Olivier wears a shirt by Theory and trousers by Neil Barrett. Opposite: He wears a sweater by Neil Barrett and corduroy trousers by Brooks Brothers.

Opposite: Olivier wears a jacket and T-shirt by Acne Studios and trousers by Corneliani.

Opposite: Olivier wears a shirt and trousers by COS. Above: He wears a jacket by Margaret Howell and a shirt by Dsquared2.

Day in The Life:
Paloma Lanna

In Barcelona, *Paloma Lanna* is beginning to branch out from the fashion empire into which she was born. Though still committed to the family business and at her mother's side day to day, Paloma is now also forging her own clothing brand—a line inspired by the muted, organic colors of Catalonia, and by the strength and softness of her longstanding Spanish sisterhood. Words by *Pip Usher* & Photography by *Marsý Hild Þórsdóttir*

"I'm inspired by art—by photography, by dance, by performance, by sculpture," says Paloma Lanna, the 27-year-old behind multidisciplinary fashion project Paloma Wool. "So I would say that clothing is the excuse to do all the artistic projects that surround it."

Those following Spanish fashion may already have spotted the growing influence of this Barcelona-based designer, whose relaxed Mediterranean aesthetic has attracted a following from the US to South Korea. Since her label launched in 2014, Paloma has produced dainty capsule collections, often in collaboration with other young artists. Signatures include linen crop tops in shades of lemon yellow and sultry maroon, creamy leather mules with a curved wooden heel, and a range of T-shirts and jackets adorned with artist Tana Latorre's scribbles of Cleopatra's reclining silhouette. The simple, somewhat ethereal aesthetic of Paloma's clothing is underscored by her campaigns, which emphasize bare backgrounds, minimal styling and a diverse mix of models that includes a woman with a stunning unibrow. For a fashion brand, it's not very fashion-y—which explains its appeal.

Wearing a black T-shirt and hoop earrings, thick hair hanging loose and wavy around her face, Paloma knows she doesn't fit the mold of the average designer. Apart from her disinterest in the glamorous aspects of fashion—she says she likes to wear her boyfriend's clothes and spend time with her cats—she has intentionally built a clothing brand with aspirations far loftier and less commercially minded than mere retail. But her freedom, in part, comes from established industry credentials. Paloma grew up privy to fashion—an only child towed along by her parents to Milan, Tokyo and New York City as they visited suppliers and gauged new trends. Perhaps she can sit slightly apart from the industry precisely because she knows it so well.

"My parents had their own brand, so I grew up surrounded by their projects and by fashion," she says. As the owners of Globe, her parents found quick success as one of the first Spanish fashion brands to start importing. ("I was told that girls decorated their school folders with photos of Globe on the front," Paloma says.) But in 1992, an economic crisis hit Spain and the Lannas' empire became too big to sustain. The business folded, the family reevaluated and, three years later, started the womenswear brand Nice Things. "It's nearly as old as I am," notes Paloma.

When it came time for university, Paloma's parents encouraged her to study business management instead of fashion design. After their own encounter with the pitfalls of entrepreneurship, they wanted her armed with the practical knowledge to run a successful business. In 2012, while Paloma was on a study exchange in New Zealand, her father died.

"We were always together, the three of us," she says of the relationship she shared with her parents. After her father's death, she joined her mother (also named Paloma) at Nice Things. Paloma and her mother—who, like her daughter, qualified in a practical subject, nursing, before diverging into fashion—remain extremely close, counting one another as confidantes and creative counsel.

Two years after she joined the family business, Paloma came to a realization. "I suddenly understood that I could do my own fashion project without being a fashion brand, that I could do something more profound than a label," she remembers. "I've always felt that I've had to follow my own path and express myself in a creative way." Her clothing line resists the rules of fashion: no seasonal collections, no mass production, no slashed prices during sales season. Instead, she crafts limited-edition capsule collections made locally from European fabrics. When an item sells out, that's it. "I don't like how the fashion industry encourages people to consume more and more," she says. "I prefer to produce in a more sustainable way."

By day, Paloma helps her mother at Nice Things—the family business. Paloma describes her mother as having "an exquisite sensitivity" and a "delicate and feminine style."

Alongside her retail offerings, Paloma showcases exploratory performance art, large-scale installations and photography. A recent project looks to ancient mythology, with a series of photographs that complements the evocative, Greek-inspired embroidery included on some of the label's clothing. The soft-focus portraits—of Paloma's friends swathed in metallic silvers and golds and gauzy robes—are as dreamlike as her fashion designs. Each subject is posed in perfect stillness, brushing their hair or gazing at their reflection in a handheld mirror—a parallel, Paloma says, between the self-absorption of the Ancient Greeks and her own generation.

Another video piece features Paloma and friends in a stark white space decorated with colored fabric and blocks of wood. Over the course of 10 minutes, they interact with their surroundings in an oddly sensual, trancelike state: Clothes come on and off, props transmute into playthings. "That was a very important project to me," she says. "It had nothing to do with designing clothes, but it was very relevant for Paloma Wool."

Browse the brand's projects and you'll see many of the same faces. Paloma's friends have always been an integral part of the business, popping up in her performance art or as collaborators on her clothing line. Many of them have been close since they were young. "I like to think of us when we were little—we were always playing and exploring and doing experiments. If we made mistakes, it was always okay and we'd laugh about them," she says. That childhood playfulness has carried over into her work today, from the relaxed design of her clothes to the equal weight granted to experimental art projects.

"I try to express with my photos, or with my pieces, that we are a group of friends doing this project," says Paloma. "We help each other, we respect ourselves, we trust ourselves, and there's a lot of love between us."

"I've always felt that I've had to follow my own path and express myself in a creative way."

Paloma's vision for her own brand extends beyond fashion and retail. In 2015, she published her first brand book, *14-14* (shown opposite), to document her various other creative pursuits and collaborations. A follow-up, *15-15*, was published this summer.

LEXICON
VIVIANE
SASSEN

ARTBEAT PUBLISHERS

naranja

paloma—wool   14—14

paloma—wool   14—14

Words by David Plaisant

Lunch with Lee

Fluted mushrooms and marshmallow-cola ice cream: the culinary talents of an American model turned war photographer turned dinner party host.

"Anyone with sense says promptly after lunch 'I always sleep after meals'."

From the famed bacchanalian feasts of ancient Rome to elaborate Victorian-era affairs to the sophisticated soirées of more modern times, the dinner party is engrained in the psyche of human sociability. Fads such as handwritten place settings may come and go, but the premise of hosting friends, acquaintances and coveted companions is here to stay.

Somewhat unorthodox guidance on this pursuit comes in the form of a new book charting the life of Lee Miller, the legendary photographer turned acclaimed photojournalist, turned cook and entertainer. *Lee Miller: A Life with Food, Friends and Recipes* is, in part, a cookbook featuring many of Miller's meticulously researched recipes.

Born in Poughkeepsie, New York in 1907, Miller left for New York City where, thanks to her striking looks, she started modeling for *Vogue* by the age of 20. Quickly finding herself at the rough end of the modeling world, she then took off to Paris, where she eventually became the assistant (and lover) of the photographer Man Ray. There, she began to acquire an understanding of fine food. It was the years during World War II, when she toured Europe photographing the impending liberation, however, that would become the most formative of her extraordinary career.

Partly traumatized by what she had seen and also restless for change, Miller's postwar life took an unexpected turn. She became pregnant with British artist and curator Roland Penrose's child, quickly divorced her Egyptian husband (she had lived in Cairo for six years in the '30s) and

gradually settled into a life split mainly between London and a farmhouse in Sussex.

The success of a dinner is, without doubt, dependent on the guests invited, and Miller's were almost unrivaled in the transatlantic artistic circles of the '50s and '60s. A cover girl, traveler, surrealist photographer (she pioneered so-called solarization technique together with Man Ray) and wartime reporter (she was famously photographed in Adolf Hitler's bathtub by David Sherman), Miller now found herself at the center of a flourishing world of contemporary art. She cooked for and entertained Picasso, Joan Miró, Henry Moore and countless others. Little surprise, then, that Miller's parties were ripe with the prerequisite of any successful dinner: "Intellectual (i.e. good) conversation was as much a necessity to her as breathing," says author Ami Bouhassane, also Miller's granddaughter.

With a rare life story and table guests that make for compelling reading on their own, it could be easy to lose sight of what this remarkable woman actually liked to cook at her now-famous meals. Thankfully, we are informed in intricately researched and lovingly told detail by the author. It quickly becomes clear that Miller was both a pioneer of international cuisine and innovative in her approach. We hear of Miller's numerous trips to the Middle East through mouthwatering excerpts taken from letters she wrote to many of her gastronomically inclined friends,

writers and fellow journalists. For instance, Miller's great friend Bettina McNulty recalls a trip to Egypt the two made in 1963: "We used that flat Arab bread, which splits, to form a hollow bowl to hold our food so had no need for plates [...] To that we added tomatoes with fresh basil. The cold soft-boiled eggs we thought at first must have been a mistake. But though hard to eat delicately, they topped off our menu perfectly. A lovely drink, called karkadeh, made by infusing hibiscus flowers, was a pink and perfect thirst quencher in the hot Egyptian sun, and it wasn't even iced."

These voyages would imbue the meals back in London and Sussex with flavors and techniques previously unknown to Miller's guests. Trips to Norway (after winning a government-funded smörgåsbord-making competition), Spain, Morocco and elsewhere, provoked sumptuously themed soirées where guests were indulged with foreign fare. Fresh from her Norwegian adventure, for example, Miller served her prize-winning dish: "Penroses' liver pate piped to look like flowers onto mushrooms that had been cooked in Madeira, butter and lemon juice then sprinkled with paprika [...] Crab mousse, Janssons Temptation, rice salad, celeriac & mussels, pate, duck salad (tongue), Swedish meatballs, new potatoes, gaffelbiter (dill and wine sauces) and salted herrings with sour cream, dill and potatoes (cold)." Aside from recipes and a very palpable sense of Miller's almost academic quest to serve the right dish, we learn of an approach to entertaining that was all her own. Meals in Sussex were the antithesis of the rigid, formal affairs that permeated the postwar period. Miller seemed to revel in the creation of a bohemian way of life for her guests; a firmly relaxed modus operandi was the order of play. In a 1951 letter to Audrey Withers, her editor at *Vogue*, Miller set out some of the rules of entertaining she had devised in Sussex. High on the list: "I don't want to spend the cocktail hour alone in the kitchen, losing my appetite from progressive tastings."

An imperative of enjoyment (both for guest and host) pervades and Miller went so far as to give advice on how to avoid that age-old post-dinner mood killer, the washing up: "Anyone with sense says promptly after lunch 'I *always* sleep after meals'. I find it immensely endearing because that's just what I am going to do myself, and tuck them away in a darkened small room."

Humor and humility, as well as an air of wry wit, comes from each page of this fascinating cookbook/anthology. Lee Miller's consummate talents as an entertainer, cook and intellectual are made vividly clear in this very personal account. Aside from the most desirable table guests of the time and her astonishing menus, there is no doubt that it was Miller's personality that was the most important ingredient to her truly delectable lunches and dinners.

Above: Dorothea Tanning, Roland Penrose, Al Lewin and Max Ernst at one of Miller's parties in 1958. Opposite: Pablo Picasso was a frequent dinner guest.

Below: Picasso at the home of Lee Miller in 1950. Opposite: Miller's original chicken fonduta recipe and her handwritten revisions.

x   PENROSE

Chicken Fonduta.

Disjoint and skin two poached 3½ lb chickens.
(See Crystal chicken) Keep them warm or reheat
in ̃foil-covered shallow serving dish, ̃which is slightly
damp̃ened wit̃h stock to keep pieces moist. Just
before serving time Drain, ~~and cover with the~~
following sauce.   *smear with the pieces with*
white truffle paste, (sold in tubes, from Italy) - & cover with
the following sauce:

~~FXMXNTAXSAXCEX~~
Fonduta Sauce.   Grate or chop, finely 1 lb.Gruyere(or Emmenth-
aler, or a mixture of both) .. into a thic̃k
bottomed enamel pan. Add 16 fluid oz. of white
wine..(fruity)   Sit in 1 teaspoon of slaked
fecule de pomme de terre, or arrowroot or corn
starch̃. ~~Bring to a boil~~ *STIRR!* lower heat and add,
as if making a liason ̃4/4̃egg yolks ̃which have
been beat̃en into 1¼ cups of light cream....

When it comes to
a boil —

Smear ~~the skinned~~ warm chicken pieces with
~~white truffle paste.(sold in tubes)..~~ and cover
with thĩs fonduta. *sauce +* ~~If~~ fresh truffles are
available put them on top of the sauce.. finely
sliced with a truffles cutter, or on a mandoline.
~~Neath~~

Cover the truffled
Chick. pieces ~~Pieces~~ *with the*

This dish is more elegant k̃using chicken breasts
only... four complete ones to make eight pieces.

parsley?

disjointed
2 3½ lbs chicken, poached + ~~disjointed~~
oz 4 complete " breasts "
Tube of white truffle paste (Italian Import)
or Fresh white truffles =
1 lb. gruyere, Emman Italian or mixture —
~~Ho~~ 2 cups fruit wine
~~Cornflo~~ 1 tbsp cornstarch or "fecule"
4 yolks , 1½ cups light cream

3
Sport

The

An American socialite swaps New York high-rise for British pastoral.

Sporting

Words by *Harriet Fitch Little* & Photography by *Pelle Crépin*

Life

Amanda Brooks was once fashion director of Barneys and a high society It Girl in New York. Then one day a rural sabbatical prompted a career epiphany. She quit the Manhattan treadmill and started a new life amid the rolling hills of the British Cotswolds, where most mornings now begin with a gallop through the countryside, jumping hedges on horseback.

Opposite: Fairgreen Farm. Previous spread: Amanda wears a coat by Ermanno Scervino, shirt by JW Anderson, trousers by Brunello Cucinelli and boots by Belstaff.

On the day I'm to meet Amanda Brooks, I wake up at 7 a.m. and scroll through Instagram with one eye open. I see she has gotten a jump on me. The American fashion maven was up at 5 a.m., on horseback by 5:30 a.m. and snapping photos of the British countryside as the sun crested over its foggy fields. Along with her 69,000 other followers, I feel I've already wasted the day by comparison.

It wasn't a good ride, Brooks admits when we meet that afternoon. She had been up all night with food poisoning, and the horse she'd borrowed from a friend and was hoping to buy had turned out to be impossibly strong. "The first field we went into, he took off. He just *flew* into the jump," she tells me, as we drive up the lane from Kingham railway station to her home at Fairgreen Farm in north Oxfordshire.

Brooks, 43, looks exceptionally composed for a woman who spent the night being sick and the morning shouting "Out of the way!" as she bowled through the Cotswolds countryside on horseback. But presumably she's a woman for whom lack of sleep barely

upper classes consider shorthand for good taste; the wallpaper is faded, the lining of the curtains spilling out. There's a huge, soppy rescue dog called Ginger shedding hair and demanding attention. Brooks often has puppies here also—fox hounds that she helps raise to run with the local hunt.

Only a handful of items hint at her past life. The sofa cushions, for example—made from vintage leopard-print coats given to Brooks by a friend. "I had pillows made out of them because I was never going to wear them," she says casually. "I don't know what you're supposed to do with leopard." I am not in a position to advise.

The story of how Brooks ended up here begins with a slipped disk and a bad case of burnout. In 2011, in Paris with Barneys for fashion week, she stepped from the curb at a funny angle and felt something jar. She spent the next few days attending shows looking, in her own words, like the Hunchback of nearby Notre-Dame, then was invalided out to New York. Down 10 pounds from the stress of a job she wasn't totally at ease in, she got shingles.

"I love English country life. I'm such a cheerleader, in typical American fashion."

registers. Five years ago, she was managing one of the most hectic schedules in retail as fashion director of Barneys New York. Back then, she was a Met Gala regular and Diane von Furstenberg's mentee. When the "patrician blonde beauty"—*The New York Times'* description—married her husband, Christopher, in 2001, it was in Louboutins designed by Christian himself (also a wedding guest). She memorably hired an intern because they could name every occasion she had appeared in *Vogue*. She once, still more memorably, turned down Mick Jagger.

But Brooks is now living the life of a farmer's wife. She's baked a cake for my arrival, and tells me she really loves making jam. "I still feel like an enthusiast, not an expert at all," she says. "But I love English country life. I'm such a cheerleader, in typical American fashion."

It's raining when we arrive at the farm, so we settle into the sitting room. It's decorated with the deliberate shabbiness that the British

Something snapped. "I think I was just more burned out than I realized. I was traveling five months a year," she says. "When I started out [in fashion], staying up until three in the morning doing a shoot was just the most exciting thing. But my priorities changed. By the time I was 30, 35, I would look around fashion shows at how many people were divorced or had never married. There are very few people on that circuit that maintain it responsibly."

Brooks decided a family sabbatical was needed—for her, her husband, Christopher, and their children, Coco (16) and Zach (14). Fairgreen was a ready-made bolthole; the farm belongs to Christopher, and sits on an estate he shares with his sister, Annabelle, and brother, Charlie—who is married to the former chief executive of News International, Rebekah Brooks.

Brooks hoped that by coming to England she might rid herself of the "mindlessness" with which she had started to view fashion.

Styling: David Nolan

Amanda and her daughter, Coco, ride through the Oxfordshire countryside most mornings. In June 2018, Amanda will publish *Farm From Home*—a memoir about life on Fairgreen Farm.

"You know when you're on a train and you're looking out the window and everything is blurry? That's how I felt," she says. She put her children in British private schools, and spent a year "making jam and riding horses."

That should have been the end of it. But Brooks arrived at Fairgreen on the crest of a wave. In 2012, public appetite for the simple life was gaining pace. Mindful living, clean eating and authenticity: The aspirations of this decade are less *Sex and the City*, more *Little House on the Prairie*. Brooks, who had actually made the transition so many dreamed of, found herself at the vanguard of a new wave of rural trendsetters. "I didn't know people had this fantasy of leaving their city life for the country," she says. Her Instagram feed switched from chic fashion to farmyard chicks (and donkeys, pigs, rabbits, lambs and horses...).

What began as a career break became a career. Five years after the move, Brooks is now rolling out her brand of British idyll; her book *Farm from Home: Stories, Insights and Recipes from a City Girl Who Moved to the Country* will be out in June 2018. The same month, she's opening a shop in the nearby market town of Stow-on-the-Wold. It's to be called Cutter & Brooks (Cutter is her maiden name) and will "curate country in a sophisticated way, from a city girl perspective," with the focus on homeware, not fashion.

"I thought I was moving to England as a break. I was moving away from what I thought was ambition and career and success," she says. "I think I just found myself feeling really at home here."

If Brooks had moved to the Cotswolds and no one had cared, would she have gotten itchy feet? "Maybe," she says. "I don't discount that in any way. The big question was if there was a way for me to feel like I was still pursuing my dreams here. The idea of retiring at 38 was just horrifying to me." She wonders out loud whether it was perhaps the sudden voguishness of country living that had made the move appealing.

Brooks can be refreshingly straightforward. When I remark that her memoir—*Always Pack a Party Dress*—paints a picture of extreme ambition, she doesn't deflect the characterization in the way women who have done very well often think necessary. "Good," she says instead. "I'm terrified of becoming complacent, so the fact that comes across is nice."

Nothing has ever happened to Brooks by accident. Aged 20, she got her first "in"—an internship with the fashion photographer Patrick Demarchelier by walking up to him in a restaurant. She got her second job—as a front-of-house "gallerina" at Gagosian—by doing the same to art mogul Larry Gagosian in a shoe shop two years later. When she decided she wanted to work for society clothing line Tuleh and they couldn't afford her, she did so in exchange for free clothes, confident she could build the brand to a point where they could.

She's still fiercely ambitious; the difference is that now, for the first time, she gets to set her own terms. "Frankly, I'd always worked for famous people, so I had a lot to say on behalf of others," she says, rattling off a list of the many times she's overhauled her appearance and even personality to fit brand style. "All the self-exploration I'd done for 20 years culminated in a place where I could stop being a chameleon, stop chasing trends."

The sniping of the New York press pack hasn't been so easy to shake. Fashion publications have enjoyed picking over Brooks' life swap, stylizing her move to the countryside as the latest indulgence in a life marked by extreme, often oblivious, privilege. As per one catty article in *The Cut*: "Her new peaceful living has allowed Brooks to free herself from stylish shackles and any sense of self-awareness."

The charge isn't totally off the mark. Brooks' early success came off the back of a Waspy Palm Beach upbringing (she met her mentor, Diane von Furstenberg, after dating her son; her college roommate at Brown was Carolina Herrera's daughter). And her rebirth into the British countryside elite has been lubricated—both socially and financially—by marriage into the family of an Eton-educated gentleman farmer. When she describes hunting on horseback, which she loves, as "the most socially inclusive activity," or later asserts that boarding school is the norm for countryside families, I'm reminded of what a snow-globe universe the Brooks family inhabits.

When we discuss this, she isn't apologetic. She recalls one article that lampooned her for telling *Vogue* she always wore designer

"I thought I was moving to England as a break. I was moving away from what I thought was ambition and career and success."

Previous spread: Amanda wears a knit by Sonia Rykiel, shirt by JW Anderson and trousers by Brunello Cucinelli.
Below: She wears a sweater by Sunspel and trousers by Ermanno Scervino.

versions of casual clothes around the farm, knowing that no one she met would be able to tell the difference. The author of the article thought this insufferably smug; Brooks disagrees. "I take ownership of that. I worked in fashion for 20 years," she says, and fetches the offending item discussed in *Vogue*—a Balmain peacoat she wears on the school run. "You could think it's from the army navy store," she says, pulling it on. Not quite, but I take the point—some people wear nice underwear to feel good about themselves; Brooks wears plain T-shirts that only she knows cost $300.

And it's clear that Brooks both loves and understands the land she's living on. She rides most days at dawn and encourages her daughter to do likewise, even though she describes the hobby as "hugely dangerous," mainly because of the jumps. "There's a way she is on a horse that I don't see in any other part of her life. She's a heroine," Brooks says by way of explanation. "Coco falling in love with horses really gave me a reason to want to be here."

She handles animals with the toughness of a farmer. Juice, the family's pet ram, was bottle-fed as a lamb and then refused to join the flock, so he lives in the kitchen garden. And when he jumps up to head-butt me she grabs him by his five-inch horns and pulls him down. It's a display of confidence impossible to fake.

In planning this meeting, we had discussed the possibility of spending the afternoon touring the farm on horseback. But the horses, when we visit them, are running in fast circles. Brooks is worried they are out of sorts and calls the groom. With her account of the morning's out-of-control steed still fresh in my mind, I suggest we might give riding a miss. Brooks, who has clearly been sizing me up, politely agrees.

Instead, she reverses a flatbed tractor out of the shed and we set off up the track. Ginger the dog runs in front of us barking; Juice the sheep runs behind bleating. "He thinks he's a dog," she explains.

The farm is on a hill that slopes down in all directions to fields below. We drive along the gallops, the open stretch of land where the horses train at speed, and I meet more of the menagerie: the hairy pigs that Zach likes to ride; the horse that rested its head in her children's laps as a foal. Brooks leans off the side of the tractor to take photos as we trundle along. "I

can also Instagram while riding a horse," she says seriously.

It is not hard to see why this lifestyle triumphed over the prospect of returning to America.

She later tells me that when she goes to New York on vacation, she carries a churning knot of anxiety around with her from touchdown to takeoff; "I felt like that for 20 years and I just didn't realize," she says.

Sometimes, she misses it. "In New York, someone was always inviting me to a party. There was always a lot of attention," she says. "[Leaving the city] you have to readjust where your confidence and self-esteem come from."

As of June 2018, it'll come from the launch of her twin projects—the book about her life on the farm, and the shop that is a reflection of it. She thinks it will be nice to have something to market other than herself. "I don't want to be using my lifestyle indefinitely for my career, so the store is sort of taking my life away from the farm."

She recalls a conversation with Net-a-Porter founder Natalie Massenet who, like Brooks, struck out on her own after a few years' hiatus. "Amanda! This is your gestation period!" Massenet told her. She is looking forward to a spring birth.

Above: Amanda wears Brunello Cucinelli. Opposite: She wears a sweater by Sunspel, shirt by Pringle, dress by JW Anderson and boots by Belstaff

David Sedaris:

Stepping Out

American humorist *David Sedaris* tracks the merits and tyranny of his Fitbit and describes how the compulsion to walk 10,000 steps (minimum) each day has led to new discoveries about life in the British countryside.

I was at an Italian restaurant in Melbourne, listening as a woman named Lesley talked about her housekeeper, an immigrant to Australia who earlier that day had cleaned the bathroom countertops with a bottle of very expensive acne medication: "She's afraid of the vacuum cleaner and can't read or write a word of English, but other than that she's marvellous."

Lesley works for a company that goes into developing countries and trains doctors to remove cataracts. "It's incredibly rewarding," she said as our antipasto plate arrived. "These are people who've been blind for years, and suddenly, miraculously, they can see again." She brought up a man who'd been operated on in a remote area of China. "They took off the bandages, and for the first time in two decades he saw his wife. Then he opened his mouth and said, 'You're so... old.'"

Lesley pushed back her shirtsleeve, and as she reached for an olive I noticed a rubber bracelet on her left wrist. "Is that a watch?" I asked.

"No," she told me. "It's a Fitbit. You synch it with your computer, and it tracks your physical activity."

I leaned closer, and as she tapped the thickest part of it a number of glowing dots rose to the surface and danced back and forth. "It's like a pedometer," she continued. "But updated, and better. The goal is to take ten thousand steps per day, and, once you do, it vibrates."

I forked some salami into my mouth. "Hard?"

"No," she said. "It's just a tingle."

A few weeks later, I bought a Fitbit of my own, and discovered what she was talking about. Ten thousand steps, I learned, amounts to a little more than four miles for someone my size—five feet five inches. It sounds like a lot, but you can cover that distance in the course of an average day without even trying, especially if you have stairs in your house, and a steady flow of people who regularly knock, wanting you to accept a package or give them directions or just listen patiently as they talk about birds, which happens from time to time when I'm home, in West Sussex, the area of England that Hugh and I live in. One April afternoon, the person at my door hoped to sell me a wooden bench. It was bought, he said, for a client whose garden he was designing. "Last week she loved it, but now she's decided to go with something else." In the bright sunlight, the fellow's hair was as orange as a Popsicle. "The company I ordered it from has a no-return policy, so I'm wondering if maybe *you'd* like to buy it." He gestured toward an unmarked van idling in front of the house, and seemed angry when I told him that I wasn't interested. "You could at least take a look before making up your mind," he said.

I closed the door a couple of inches. "That's O.K." Then, because it's an excuse that works for just about everything, I added, "I'm American."

"Meaning?" he said.

"We... stand up a lot," I told him.

"Oldest trick in the book," my neighbor Thelma said when I told her what had happened. "That bench was stolen from someone's garden, I guarantee it."

This was seconded by the fellow who came to empty our septic tank. "Pikeys," he said.

"Come again?"

"Tinkers," he said. "Pikeys."

"That means Gypsies," Thelma explained, adding that the politically correct word is "travellers."

I was travelling myself when I got my Fitbit, and because the tingle feels so good, not just as a sensation but also as a mark of accomplishment, I began pacing the airport rather than doing what I normally do, which is sit in the waiting area, wondering which of the many people around me will die first, and of what. I also started taking the stairs instead of the escalator, and avoiding the moving sidewalk.

"Every little bit helps," my old friend Dawn, who frequently eats lunch while hula-hooping and has been known to visit her local Y three times a day, said. She had a Fitbit as well, and swore by it. Others I met weren't quite so taken. These were people who had worn one until the battery died. Then, rather than recharging it, which couldn't be simpler, they'd stuck it in a drawer, most likely with all the other devices they'd lost interest in over the years. To people like Dawn and me, people who are obsessive to begin with, the Fitbit is a digital trainer, perpetually egging us on. During the first few weeks that I had it, I'd return to my hotel at the end of the day, and when I discovered that I'd taken a total of, say, twelve thousand steps, I'd go out for another three thousand.

"But why?" Hugh asked when I told him

about it. "Why isn't twelve thousand enough?"

"Because," I told him, "my Fitbit thinks I can do better."

I look back at that time and laugh—fifteen thousand steps—Ha! That's only about seven miles! Not bad if you're on a business trip or you're just getting used to a new prosthetic leg. In Sussex, though, it's nothing. Our house is situated on the edge of a rolling downland, a perfect position if you like what the English call "rambling." I'll follow a trail every now and then, but as a rule I prefer roads, partly because it's harder to get lost on a road, but mainly because I'm afraid of snakes. The only venomous ones in England are adders, and even though they're hardly ubiquitous, I've seen three that had been run over by cars. Then I met a woman named Janine who was bitten and had to spend a week in the hospital. "It was completely my own fault," she said. "I shouldn't have been wearing sandals."

"It didn't *have* to strike you," I reminded her. "It could have just slid away."

Janine was the type who'd likely blame herself for getting mugged. "It's what I get for having anything worth taking!" she'd probably say. At first, I found her attitude fascinating. Then I got vindictive on her behalf, and started carrying a snake killer, or, at least, something that could be used to grab one by the neck and fling it into the path of an oncoming car. It's a hand-size claw on a pole, and was originally designed for picking up litter. With it I can walk, fear snakes a little less, and satisfy my insane need

for order all at the same time. I've been cleaning the roads in my area of Sussex for three years now, but before the Fitbit I did it primarily on my bike, and with my bare hands. That was fairly effective, but I wound up missing a lot. On foot, nothing escapes my attention: a potato-chip bag stuffed into the hollow of a tree, an elderly mitten caught in the embrace of a blackberry bush, a mud-coated matchbook at the bottom of a ditch. Then, there's all the obvious stuff: the cans and bottles and great greasy sheets of paper that fish-and-chips comes wrapped in. You can tell where my territory ends and the rest of England begins. It's like going from the rose arbor in Sissinghurst to Fukushima after the tsunami. The difference is staggering.

Since getting my Fitbit, I've seen all kinds of things I wouldn't normally have come across. Once, it was a toffee-colored cow with two feet sticking out of her. I was rambling that afternoon, with my friend Maja, and as she ran to inform the farmer I marched in place, envious of the extra steps she was getting in. Given all the time I've spent in the country, you'd think I might have seen a calf being born, but this was a first for me. The biggest surprise was how unfazed the expectant mother was. For a while, she lay flat on the grass, panting. Then she got up and began grazing, still with those feet sticking out.

"Really?" I said to her. "You can't go *five minutes* without eating?"

Around her were other cows, all of whom

seemed blind to her condition.

"Do you think she knows there's a baby at the end of this?" I asked Maja after she'd returned. "A woman is told what's going to happen in the delivery room, but how does an animal interpret this pain?"

I thought of the first time I had a kidney stone. That was in New York, in 1991, back when I had no money or health insurance. All I knew was that I was hurting, and couldn't afford to do anything about it. The night was spent moaning. Then I peed blood, followed by what looked like a piece of gravel from an aquarium. That's when I put it all together.

What might I have thought if, after seven hours of unrelenting agony, a creature the size of a full-grown cougar emerged, inch by inch, from the hole at the end of my penis and started hassling me for food? Was that what the cow was going through? Did she think she was dying, or had instinct somehow prepared her for this?

Maja and I watched for an hour. Then the sun started to set, and we trekked on, disappointed. I left for London the next day, and when I returned several weeks later, and hiked back to the field, I saw mother and child standing side by side, not in the loving way that I had imagined but more like strangers waiting for the post office to open. Other animals I've seen on my walks are foxes and rabbits. I've stumbled upon deer, stoats, a hedgehog, and more pheasants than I could possibly count. All the badgers I find are dead, run over by cars and eventually feasted upon by carrion-eating

"At the end of my first sixty-thousand-step day, I staggered home with my flashlight knowing that there will be no end to it until my feet snap off at the ankles. Why is it that some people can manage a thing like a Fitbit, while others go off the rails and allow it to rule, and perhaps even ruin, their lives? "

slugs, which are themselves eventually flattened, and feasted upon by other slugs.

Back when Maja and I saw the cow, I was averaging twenty-five thousand steps, or around ten and a half miles per day. Trousers that had grown too snug were suddenly loose again, and I noticed that my face was looking a lot thinner. Then I upped it to thirty thousand steps, and started moving farther afield. "We saw David in Arundel picking up a dead squirrel with his grabbers," the neighbors told Hugh. "We saw him outside Steyning rolling a tire down the side of the road"; " . . . in Pulborough dislodging a pair of Y-fronts from a tree branch." Before the Fitbit, once we'd eaten dinner I was in for the evening. Now, though, as soon as I'm finished with the dishes I walk to the pub and back, a distance of 3,895 steps. There are no street lights where we live, and the houses I pass at 11 p.m. are either dark or very dimly lit. I often hear owls, and the flapping of woodcocks disturbed by the beam of my flashlight. One night, I heard a creaking sound, and noticed that the minivan parked a dozen or so steps ahead of me was rocking back and forth. A lot of people where we live seem to have sex in their cars. I know this because I find their used condoms, sometimes on the road but more often just off it, in little pull-over areas. In addition to spent condoms, in one of the spots that I patrol I regularly pick up empty KFC containers and a great number of soiled Handi Wipes. Do they eat fried chicken and *then* have sex, or is it the other way round? I wonder.

I look back on the days I averaged only thirty thousand steps, and think, Honestly, how lazy can you get? When I hit thirty-five thousand steps a day, Fitbit sent me an e-badge, and then one for forty thousand, and forty-five thousand. Now I'm up to sixty thousand, which is twenty-five and a half miles. Walking that distance at the age of fifty-seven, with completely flat feet while lugging a heavy bag of garbage, takes close to nine hours—a big block of time, but hardly wasted. I listen to audiobooks, and podcasts. I talk to people. I learn things: the fact, for example, that, in the days of yore, peppercorns were sold individually and, because they were so valuable, to guard against theft the people who packed them had to have their pockets sewed shut.

At the end of my first sixty-thousand-step day, I staggered home with my flashlight knowing that I'd advance to sixty-five thousand, and that there will be no end to it until my feet snap off at the ankles. Then it'll just be my jagged bones stabbing into the soft ground. Why is it some people can manage a thing like a Fitbit, while others go off the rails and allow it to rule, and perhaps even ruin, their lives? While marching along the roadside, I often think of a TV show that I watched a few years back—*Obsessed*, it was called. One of the episodes was devoted to a woman who owned two treadmills, and walked like a hamster on a wheel from the moment she got up until she went to bed. Her family would eat dinner, and she'd observe them from her vantage point beside the table,

panting as she asked her children about their day. I knew that I was supposed to scoff at this woman, to be, at the very least, entertainingly disgusted, the way I am with the people on *Hoarders*, but instead I saw something of myself in her. Of course, she did her walking on a treadmill, where it served no greater purpose. So it's not like we're *really* that much alike. Is it?

In recognition of all the rubbish I've collected since getting my Fitbit, my local council is naming a garbage truck after me. The fellow in charge e-mailed to ask which font I would like my name written in, and I answered Roman.

"Get it?" I said to Hugh. "*Roamin'*."

He lost patience with me somewhere around the thirty-five-thousand mark, and responded with a heavy sigh. Shortly after I decided on a typeface, for reasons I cannot determine my Fitbit died. I was devastated when I tapped the broadest part of it and the little dots failed to appear. Then I felt a great sense of freedom. It seemed that my life was now my own again. But was it? Walking twenty-five miles, or even running up the stairs and back, suddenly seemed pointless, since, without the steps being counted and registered, what use were they? I lasted five hours before I ordered a replacement, express delivery. It arrived the following afternoon, and my hands shook as I tore open the box. Ten minutes later, my new master strapped securely around my left wrist, I was out the door, racing, practically running, to make up for lost time. *This essay originally appeared in a 2014 issue of* The New Yorker.

Athletes are champions on the field, and of larger issues on the world stage. Photography by *Robin Broadbent*

SPORT:
Proxy Warriors
Silence
Word Play
Gender Gaps

Jump rope: Hock Design

Words by Alex Anderson

Proxy Warriors

George Orwell famously referred to modern global sport as "war minus the shooting." In this view, sport enacts larger political conflicts, and world-class athletes become both spirited performers and fierce partisans—proxy warriors whose successes or failures reverberate far beyond the field of competition. These echoes are loudest at moments of great tension, when war may be unthinkable but competing sides crave victory and vindication over their rivals. On the most prominent stage for international competition, the athletes of the modern Olympics compete at the apogee of their sports while they engage the great political and social struggles of our age. The most powerful images of these competitors convey a fascinating balance of ferocity and beauty and show athletes not merely as combatants but as men and women striving to advance the ideals of humanity.

When *Sports Illustrated* asked readers in 2014 to vote on its "most iconic" cover of the previous 60 years, the readers chose its depiction of the US Olympic hockey team's 1980 victory over the USSR in Lake Placid. Heinz Kluetmeier's photograph captured a moment of tumultuous jubilation after the final buzzer. Some athletes embraced; others lifted arms and sticks in victory; still others sprawled on the ice, their skates and gloves pointing inelegantly skyward. A fan's American flag waved over the commotion. Hardly reminiscent of classical statues of Olympic javelin or discus throwers, it instead conveyed the breathless, spontaneous joy

of victory at a moment of global dread. Everyone watching the Cold War rivals witnessed more than an athletic contest; and the photograph captured a collective exuberance that felt heroic and historic, at least for Americans.

Twelve years earlier in Mexico City, two African-American sprinters stood momentarily victorious but resolutely engaged in the continuing global struggle of the oppressed. John Dominis photographed gold medalist Tommie Smith and bronze medalist John Carlos with bowed heads and powerfully raised fists, one left and one right. They were offering what Carlos described in his autobiography as a "human rights salute" (widely, but erroneously, reported as a "Black Power" salute) to the world. The overtly political gesture came at great cost—resulting in the athletes' ejection from the games and intense criticism in the US—but forcefully captured personal triumph subsumed by national and global apprehensions.

Fanny Blankers-Koen had engaged in a similar struggle as she competed for four gold medals at the 1948 London Olympics. Although the International Athletics Association named the versatile Dutch runner "woman athlete of the 20th century" in 1999, the world knew her, sometimes derisively, as "The Flying Housewife." Critics questioned her for "selfishly" racing instead of constantly mothering her two children and for competing in front of the world at the advanced age of 30 "in short trousers." A later description of Blankers-Koen as "A Queen with Man's Legs" (the

title of a 2003 biography by Kees Kooman), proffers a no less paradoxical image of an athlete whom photographs show ferociously breaking Olympic finish lines, every leg muscle etched in beautiful intensity. It exemplifies a persistent and troubling incongruity described by sociologists Ali Bowes and Alan Bairner in their recent study of elite British women athletes. They found that these athletes often feel compelled to "develop characteristics associated with masculinity," and to define their femininity "in contrast to, and apart from, sport." In her early victories, Blankers-Koen represented not just the Netherlands, but also the ongoing effort of all women in sport to gain equivalence as athletes.

Understanding that Olympians symbolize something larger than sport, reggae artist Ziggy Marley calls his Jamaican countryman Usain Bolt "a unifying force." "Usain Bolt is a light," he told *TIME* magazine, and a global generation of ordinary people can look up to this brilliant athlete, whose own modest upbringing and lack of artifice make him one of them. Christian Petersen's joyous 2012 portrait of Bolt after a world record-setting sprint in Beijing captures this humanity, as well as the ancient perfection of the Olympic ideal. With one knee on the ground, waist and shoulders counterpoised, eyes forward, Bolt casts his perfectly formed arms diagonally skyward in happy victory. This iconic photo is a reminder that we admire Olympians not just for their athletic prowess, but also because they carry historic burdens.

Words by Charles Shafaieh

Basketball: Nike Versa Tack

Silence

In March 2017, an experiment was conducted during an NBA game at New York City's Madison Square Garden: For the first half of the basketball game, no extraneous noise—from music to cheerleading—was permitted, so that spectators and players could "experience the game in its purest form." "Enjoy the sounds of the game," the Jumbotron implored. Pleasure, however, was scarce in the cavernous area. Rather, the soundtrack of squeaky shoes and hushed murmurings from the crowd produced what many called an unnerving, eerie effect.

For those at home with television and radio, the cacophony that today overwhelms most sporting events is dominated by the sportscaster's commentary—a seemingly all-knowing voice describing, with startling immediacy, the play-by-play of bodies colliding and balls flying across courts and fields. A form of simultaneous translation, this near-constant speech requires immense concentration as well as deep-seated knowledge of the sport and individual athletes. Unlike news anchors, whose measured delivery creates confidence and engenders trust in the viewer, sportscasters become ideal companions of a sort to those listening: They provide informative reportage but, like rapt fans, their voices—in tempo, rhythm and volume—often emulate the tenor of the match, increasing tension for spectators as their speech quickens and audibly sharing the audience's joys and, at times, frustrations.

But as with any translation, the chosen words have consequences. A 25-year study by Purdue University's Cheryl Cook and University of Southern California's Michela Musto and Michael A. Messner found that commentary often exhibits "gender bland sexism" in which "'matter-of-fact' reactions… [suggest to listeners] that women's sports lack the excitement and interest of men's sports." All mediation directs and distorts, making it critical not just how prime the view is from one's seat but also the soundscape to which it exposes you.

Whether *fumbling* or *chomping at the bit, dealing a low blow* or *reaching a stalemate*, idioms with origins in sports and games fill the English language. Baseball, boxing and football led to numerous phrases—*touching base, letting down your guard* and *dropping the ball*, respectively—but other, often surprising, games also maintain a steady presence in the vernacular. About fox hunting, Oscar Wilde said, "The English country gentleman galloping after the fox—the unspeakable in full pursuit of the uneatable." And yet the controversial activity is referenced whenever *red herrings* arise: A 17th-century text on horse training refers to the practice of using smoked fish when training horses to follow dogs that are chasing a scent. (Its current meaning dates to 1807.) Perhaps even more surprising is the linguistic retention of another ancient sport: cockfighting. *Crestfallen, cocky* and *well-heeled* all derive from this violent competition, in addition to *cockpits* and the *pecking order*.

Sports-inflected language infuses contemporary corporate culture, imbuing it with a sense of competition and a winner-takes-all mentality. Even a *heavy hitter* may come across a *sticky wicket* (i.e. a difficult problem, derived from the challenges endured when playing on a wicket, or wet cricket pitch). Or your favorite *sparring partner* may *throw in the towel*. Or *take off the gloves* or *get the ball rolling* or *hit below the belt*. When *bull's-eyes, slam dunks, curveballs* and *strikeouts* become the way of describing countless events, the workplace—and society, through a ripple effect—becomes a playing field occupied by winners and losers.

Sports permeating critical facets of life is not new: St. Paul, in his letters, frequently uses sport as a metaphor for good Christian behavior. "Everyone who competes in the games goes into strict training," he writes to the Corinthians. "They do it to get a crown that will not last, but we do it to get a crown that will last forever."

Word Play

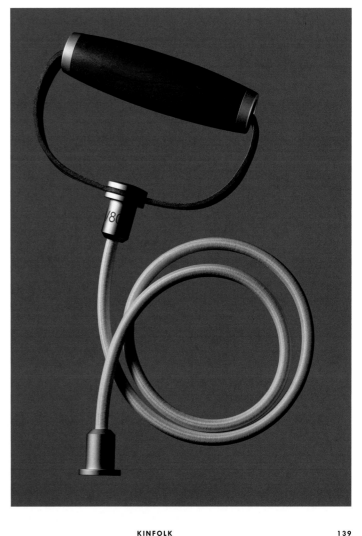

Words by Charles Shafaieh

Extender: Hock Design; Overleaf: Training band: Bollinger

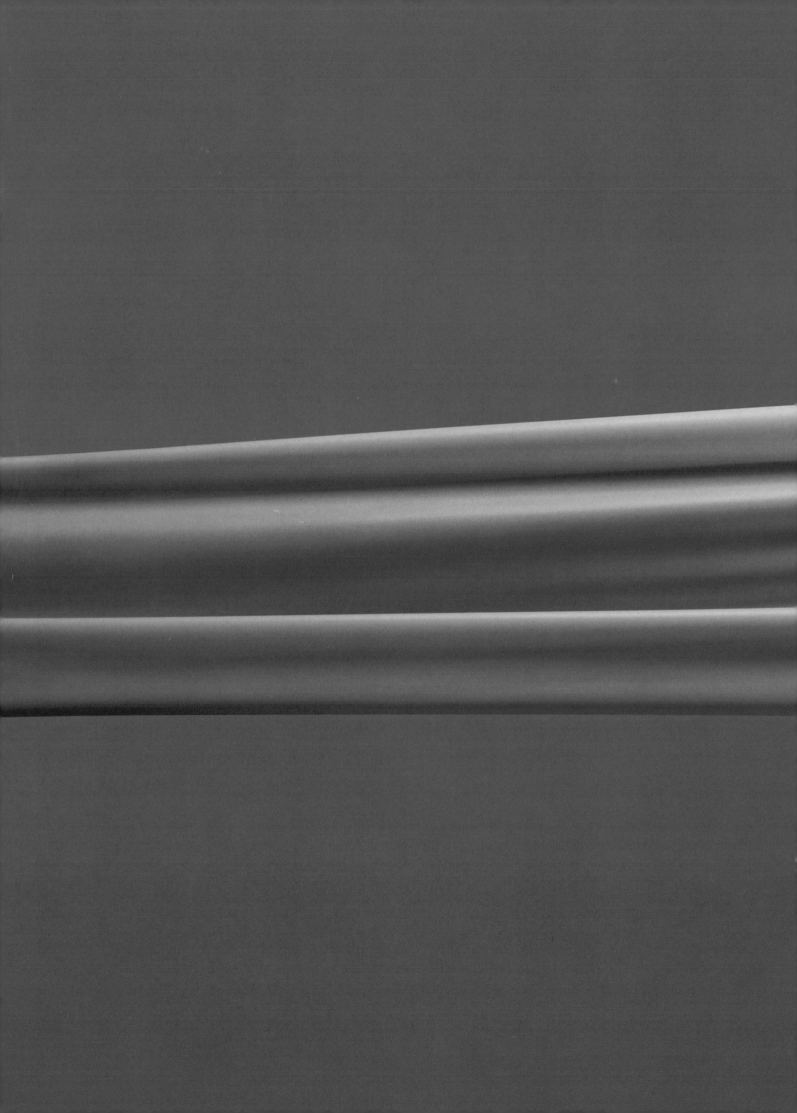

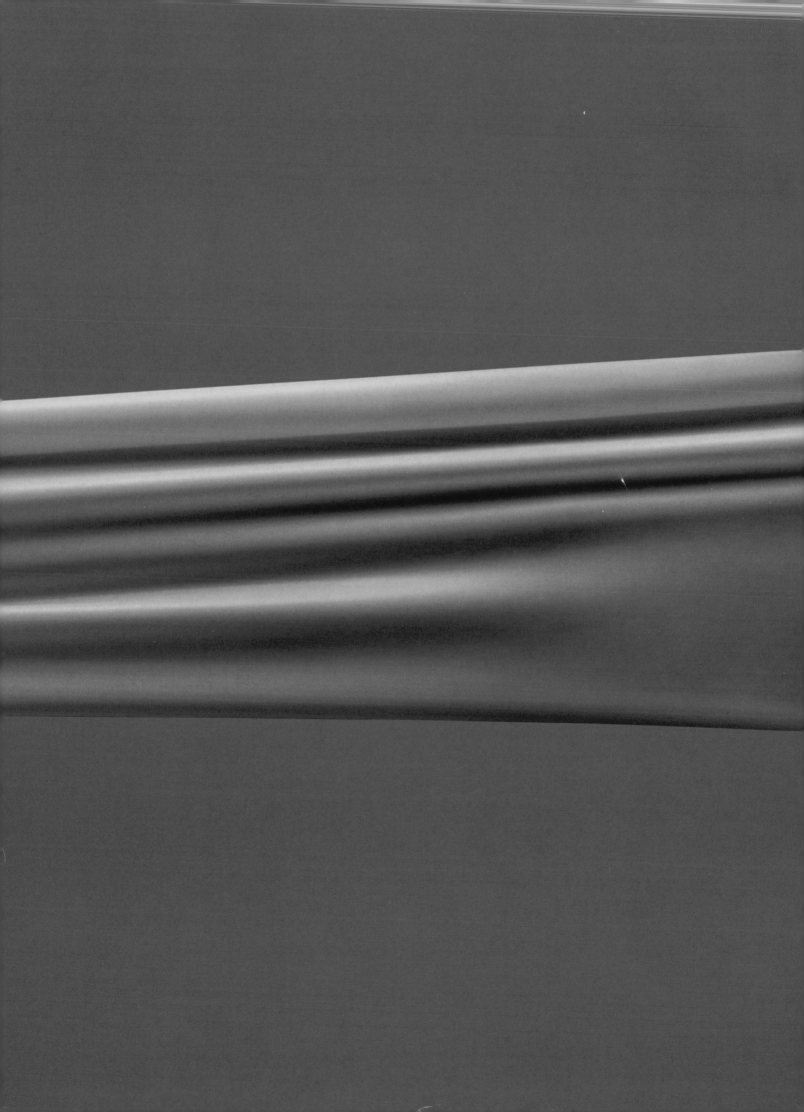

Words by Shireen Ahmed

Gender Gaps

All over the world, professional women athletes are struggling for recognition and for basic needs like equipment, support from national federations and, most importantly, pay equity. In football (in the US, soccer), for example, women are paid a fraction of what their male counterparts earn. For comparison, the United States women's national team was awarded $2 million for winning the Women's World Cup in 2015; the year before, the men's team received $8 million for just making the round of 16. But the imbalance between the genders extends far beyond the issue of equal pay.

Hajra Khan is captain of Pakistan's national women's soccer team. This year, her team was forced to withdraw from SAFF—the major regional tournament—because the Pakistan Football Federation claimed they didn't have enough money for a women's training camp or to send the players to India for the competition. Khan is the first woman from Pakistan to play internationally. "We waited two years to play in this championship, but now all we can do is sit at home and watch the matches from our lounges. It is really disappointing. The PFF is ruining our careers," Khan told *The Express Tribune* in Pakistan.

In April, the Irish women's team pushed back and refused to train. Many team members had been obliged to take other jobs to support themselves and their families, but the final straw came when they were asked to change in airport washrooms and immediately hand back uniforms to the Football Association of Ireland after the competition. In Argentina, the women's soccer team also declared a strike earlier this year, demanding basics like timely wages, proper grass fields and adequate transportation. The team had traveled third-class on a bus for hours before a match in Uruguay, and the federation had made no hotel arrangements. In 2012, the Japanese women's soccer team—also Women's World Cup champions—flew in economy while the men's team traveled in first class.

The lack of equality and respect is not always reported in mainstream media and can escape the public's notice. Meanwhile, limited media coverage of the teams becomes a factor in how much leagues and federations will promote and protect their women athletes. Inadequate support not only impedes the development of female athletes, but can also be used as a political tool that prevents them from competing as they should. This is doubly unfair to the players whose only motive is to play the sport they love.

After they won the Women's World Cup in 2015, the United States women's national team made headlines with the #EqualPlay-EqualPay campaign when they challenged the US Soccer Federation and the collective bargaining agreement for better pay. Some of the players at the forefront of the campaign—Megan Rapinoe, Hope Solo, Becky Sauerbrunn, Alex Morgan and Carli Lloyd—are the most recognizable in the world. Personal posts on social media explained their case and loyal fans supported them. The team fired and replaced the head of their players' union in order to intensify advocacy for their goals. More than a year later, the two parties reached a deal. By putting a spotlight on equity issues, the US women's team's efforts help thousands of players globally.

Around the world, women's teams are challenging gender discrimination. In December 2016, Nigeria's national forward, Asisat Oshoala, led the Super Falcons in a team sit-in when the African champions were not paid any of the money they were promised for winning. They were also owed money from the Nigeria Football Federation for qualifying for the tournament they won. "We are tired of the lies and false promises from the NFF," a player (requesting anonymity) told the BBC. The message to women and girls is to not settle and to push back against the male-dominated establishment. Grassroots organizations like Discover Football, Women in Football, Equal Playing Field and FareNet are engaged in the ongoing battle to create spaces for women and girls to develop and to be educated on their rights.

Many federations around the world claim to support women in soccer, girl's development, and elevation of the sport and yet can't seem to pay their players. It's a vicious cycle where women are expected to train mercilessly—and win—in order to get solid and consistent financial backing. But they can't win unless the basic training requirements are met. On local, regional and national teams, women and girls need proper support and respect as they train, to grow as players and individuals. It is a heavy burden to ask aspiring players—or world champions—to fight both off the field and on it. Solidarity from male allies is crucial as is increased women's representation as coaches, officials and executives at all levels of the game.

Every day more girls take up the game. And when we see more women in soccer boardrooms and see players being cheered by not only their families but by their federations, we will make sustainable change.

Cork blocks: Outdoor Voices

The

Gymnastics is one of the most physically demanding sports for the human body. To perform it with grace requires equal parts physical strength and mental focus. Photography by *Pelle Crépin* & Styling by *David Nolan*

Gym

Previous Spread: Dennis wears trousers and braces by Anderson & Sheppard. Above: He wears a glove by Budd and a sweater by Moncler.
Opposite: Luke wears a sweater by JW Anderson and trousers by Neil Barrett.

Dennis wears head-to-toe Margaret Howell.

Opposite: Dennis wears a shirt by Ermenegildo Zegna and trousers by Loewe.

Opposite: Luke wears shorts by Moncler. Above: Dennis wears a sweater from Ermenegildo Zegna.

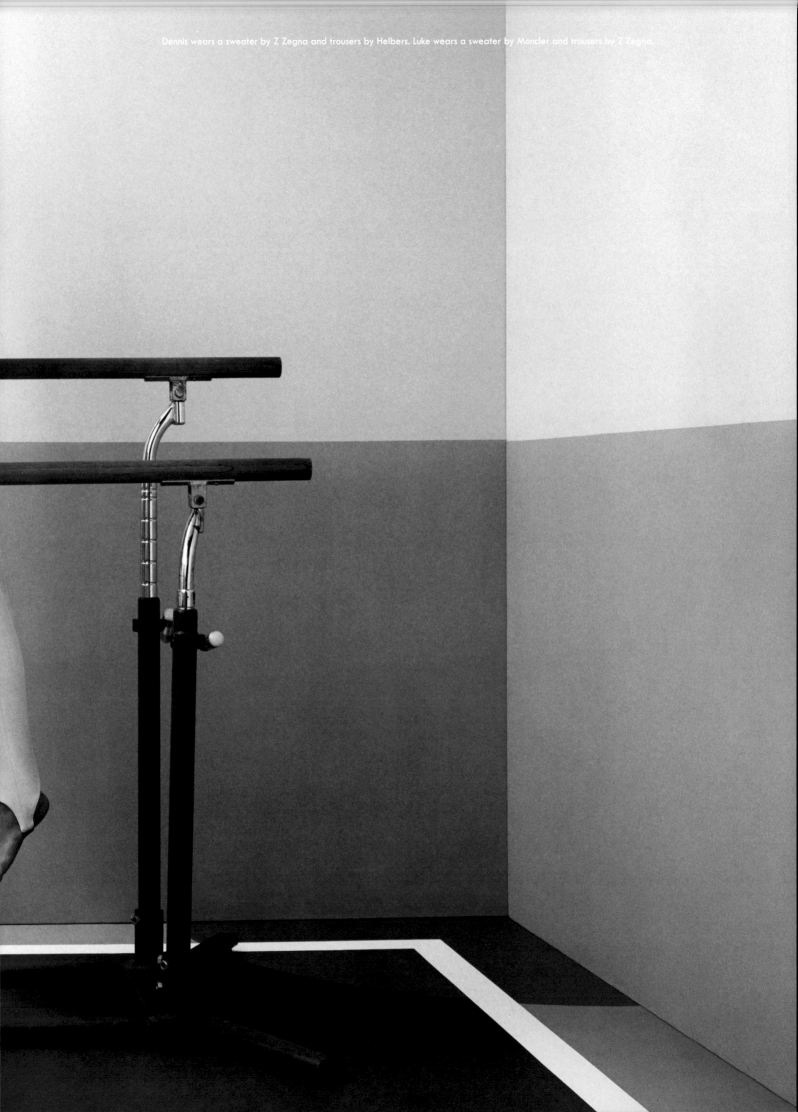

Above: Luke wears Neil Barrett head-to-toe. Opposite: He wears shorts by Orlebar Brown.

Dennis wears a suit by Dsquared2 and sneakers by Canali. Luke wears a suit by Sandro and sneakers by Helbers.

The History of Bad Advice

When I was working at a newspaper in Phnom Penh a few years ago, my Cambodian colleague went on a no ice diet. It was the hottest part of the year and our office ran on sweet iced coffees by day and iced beers by night. She refused both, as did many Cambodian women that year. Ice, she explained when asked, provided an unwelcome shock to the metabolism and therefore slowed it down.

When you encounter a fad diet whose logic you are unfamiliar with, its ridiculousness slaps you in the face. And yet at the exact same time as Cambodian women were sweating their way through the summer months, American and European media outlets were lending serious credence to another ice diet evangelist. According to the American gastroenterologist Brian Weiner, anyone hoping to lose weight shouldn't cut out ice, they should eat enormous quantities of it. His logic, as reported by respectable publications including *The Atlantic* and *The Times*, also sounded vaguely plausible: Cold things take more energy to burn, so eating ice must make your body work harder.

"I earnestly hope not to get lumped in with the counter-productive fad diet promoters," Weiner wrote on the website where he laid out the scheme. His words are strikingly like those of another North American diet guru whose star rose a century earlier. Launching his campaign for a diet pill called Figuroids in 1907, Canadian doctor George Dixon sought to reassure his skeptical public by saying, "Probably you have tried obesity cures which have seriously injured your stomach and alarmed you and your friends. In Figuroids, you have a genuine cure." His claim (that the pill would dissolve fat cells) was patently ridiculous. But every diet guru knows that to assert their authenticity as the true weight-loss messiah they must begin by dismissing as quacks the long line of hopefuls who've come before them.

Dieting has existed for as long as people have lived in groups in which at least a minority of people have more food than they need to survive. Sometimes, those diets have been sensible: As with so many things, the Ancient Greeks seemed to have got it about right when they counseled overweight people to eat more plants and less meat. But for the most part, when it comes to weight, we seem to be irrepressibly drawn to quick fixes and strange fads.

Perhaps it's because body shape is somewhat mysterious. Unlike quack cures for diseases, which will quickly prove their inefficacy, the success of a diet isn't cut and dried. "Diets are a particularly easy thing for people to promote because there's this idea that you can blame the individual if they don't stick to it," says Caroline Rance, medical historian and author of *The Quack Doctor*. And clearly certain fad diets do work in the short term. I have no doubt that my Cambodian colleague lost weight when she cut out ice, if only because she stopped drinking five servings of condensed milk per day as a result of it.

Louise Foxcroft, author of *Calories & Corsets: A History of Dieting over 2000 Years*, takes a sociological position when tracing the roots of our obsession. We diet, she says, because "it's so visual and so obvious." "[In Christian culture] it goes back to one of the seven deadly sins, which is gluttony—your sin is written on your body in excess flesh for everyone to see."

Prior to the modern period, Foxcroft says, the dominant association with dieting was a religious one. At a time when food was simply a source of fuel, the people who had the most reason to fret over it were those for whom the very idea of having a body was unwelcome. St. Paul asked the early Christians to "mortify the ways of nature" to honor God, and the early aesthetes seized on his words as a cue to fast, or eat only sparse meals, or in some cases stop eating altogether. Self-denial as a sign of godliness is an association that still exists today. Most major religions have nominated periods of fasting as emblems of devotion—Ramadan, Yom Kippur, Lent, Maha Shivaratri. Of course, rich people had to worry about their waistlines

The diet industry mines the deep seam of emotion that surrounds our eating habits to sell a precision-calibrated hope that morality, appearance, lifestyle, wellness—almost anything, really—can be improved if only we put different things in our mouth. Such advice usually nourishes insecurity more than it does the body. It turns out that the history of bad dieting advice is long and strange and full of charlatans out to profit from our gullibility. It's also a perfect example of the old adage, "The more things change, the more they stay the same." *Harriet Fitch Little examines its evolution.*

for more prosaic reasons. Often their solutions were extreme. The Roman statesman Cato the Elder recommended that portly senators eat only cabbage soup and drink the urine of cabbage soup enthusiasts. Writing in *De Agri Cultura*, the oldest surviving work of Latin prose, he counseled that the vegetable "promotes digestion marvelously and is an excellent laxative, and the urine is wholesome for everything." When William the Conqueror got fat, his solution was to sleep as much as possible and consume only alcohol—a foreshadowing of the Sleeping Beauty diet currently being promoted in the media by Dr. Michael Breus, who believes that extreme weight loss can be achieved by simply sleeping more. Luigi Cornaro, born in Venice in 1484, was perhaps the first diet book author. In *The Art of Living Long*, he advised people to limit themselves to 12 ounces of food and 14 ounces of wine per day. When he got old, he limited his daily intake to a single egg. It seems he hit on something—Cornaro lived to be almost 100.

Foxcroft points out that until the industrial revolution, most people were eating healthily by default: a lot of vegetables and a bit of meat. "For most of the population that's all they could afford to eat anyway, so they were largely doing the right thing," says Foxcroft. "Dieting was for the elite, and it trick-

led down to the poor over the centuries." Rance, who works primarily on British history, pinpoints the shift as occurring in the early Victorian era. "During the 19th century, rural populations migrated to the towns and that probably changed people's diets to a certain extent. They were eating more sugar, more processed food. It became easier to become fat even if you didn't have much money." Like so many things in this field, she says it's hard to separate cause and effect. She suspects that the fact that poor people were getting fatter pushed the wealthy to covet slimmer figures because there was no longer a social cachet attached to having curves.

According to Rance, the first wave of modern dieting innovations was for the most part quite sensible, requiring weight-loss hopefuls to stick to strict plans. "I think in the earlier part of the Victorian era, the idea of self-discipline and control was part of what was fueling that interest in taking control of your body," she says.

Rance cites English undertaker William Banting as the most obvious example of this fashion for self-denial. In 1864, Banting published *Letter on Corpulence*, in which he laid out the first systematized low-carbohydrate, high-protein diet—a forerunner of the Atkins. The diet, which he called "simply miraculous," became an international phenomenon. In *Calories &*

Corsets, Foxcroft reports that *banting* is still used as a synonym for dieting in Sweden. It makes sense that the word has lingered there: The country made headlines in 2014 when it became the first to officially endorse a high-fat, low-carb plan as part of its national health care system.

Thirty years after *Letter on Corpulence* hit the shelves, an American stole Banting's crown. Horace Fletcher, nicknamed "the great masticator," found widespread acclaim for his health plan that recommended chewing food until it became liquid before swallowing it. He advocated roughly 100 chews per bite, with a bit of onion taking more than 10 minutes to swallow. The idea was disgusting, and its science was fanciful (he thought there was a "filter mechanism" in the mouth and that chewing food would allow it to work more efficiently). But as a diet "Fletcherism" was a resounding success—eating became such a long and unpleasant ordeal that those attempting it quickly shed pounds. But even faddish Fletcherism couldn't compete with the new wave of diet gurus. As the 19th century welcomed a series of seemingly miraculous scientific discoveries—anesthesia, pasteurization and x-rays among them—the public became increasingly confident that an obesity cure would soon figure on the list of breakthroughs. It never did, but that didn't stop the quacks. "There was a lot of hope that diseases could be cured if you could find the one specific thing that will kill some particular bacteria," explains Rance. "It gave people the opportunity to come in and say, 'Obesity is a disease and we have the cure.' That was probably very appealing."

Talk of science and innovation became the go-to language of commercial persuasion. "For example, in the adverts for Russell's anti-corpulent medication they would talk about people like Louis Pasteur and his discovery [of pasteurization], and reference the fact that they had also made an amazing discovery," says Rance. "For pretty much anything that was wrong with you, you could probably find a patent remedy that would cure it. You could see the beginning of the 20th century as a Golden Age of quackery."

Some of the new supplements were harmless. Russell's anti-corpulent medication contained little aside from citric acid, so mild heartburn was likely the only downside of taking it. The same was true of the many "reducing soaps" on offer—heavily marketed mail-order products that claimed to destroy fat when rubbed on the offending area. The only thing the soaps damaged was the purchaser's bank balance. This was the "electric era" and doctors got in on the act with electric belts. Said to aid weight loss (as well as everything from kidney problems to impotency), their currents were

so low they barely registered on galvanometers. But other inventions were positively dangerous. Arsenic, strychnine and ammonia were all presented as "miracle cures" to be either consumed or rubbed on the body. Rubber underwear, believed to force the body to sweat more, lead to bacterial infections and skin decay. Perhaps most disturbingly, several accounts suggest that tapeworm eggs were regularly consumed: The tapeworm would hatch inside the stomach, eat whatever the dieter ate, then (somehow) be removed. But Rance maintains that there's little solid evidence that this particular fad was ever popular, or even that it existed. She points out that by the turn of the 20th century, medical bodies had started to make serious attempts at regulation: "If charlatans had been selling tapeworm pills, these authorities would surely have been down on their heads so hard they'd have been nibbling their own intestinal walls."

One trend whose existence is unfortunately incontestable is the cigarette diet. In the early 20th century, Lucky Strike began explicitly marketing to overweight people, particularly women. They ran advertising campaigns that showed women in bikinis casting off their portly shadows, accompanied by the slogan "Reach for a Lucky instead of a sweet." The women in the ads were fun-loving and free—role models for a generation of increasingly independent women.

Whether weight loss was ever a tool for women's liberation is a murkier question than it might seem. Foxcroft makes the case that in several countries the turn toward boyish figures for women came during wartime. "It was quite the thing to be flat-chested and boyish when there were so few boys left," she writes. Foxcroft argues that women chose to mimic the figures of men to assert their equality: While anti-suffragists insisted that a woman's place was in the home, those who sought the vote proved their worth by adopting men's silhouettes. Both Foxcroft and Rance are unwilling to be drawn on whether women were instigators or dupes of the new diet industry. As Foxcroft puts it: "It's patronizing to say that women are victims, but it's supply and demand, isn't it? The increasing demand certainly brought more people into the market producing their powders and their crystal bracelets." The veil of history has descended on an industry where facts were already murky, often absent entirely.

Today, the diet industrial complex shows no signs of losing its grip. It would be impossible to present a comprehensive survey of the various prescriptions that our contemporary quacks have trumpeted, and boring to attempt it—fads are consigned to the bargain bin so quickly that listing them is like trying to recall the past winners of your favorite reality TV show. Rance points out that the landscape is more fertile for fads today than at any

"Dieting has existed for as long as people have lived in groups in which at least a minority of people have more food than they need to survive. Sometimes, those diets have been sensible. But for the most part, when it comes to weight, we seem to be irrepressibly drawn to quick fixes and strange fads."

point in the last century: The internet has reintroduced an unregulated marketplace of options for potion pushers looking to prove that "their particular brand of alternative remedy will cure everything."

One thing that is remarkable is our apparent lack of imagination. Researching the history of dieting, you notice that every new fad diet has a centuries-old precedent: the Atkins diet has its origins in Banting; the Paleo diet—which encourages participants to only eat things they would have been able to access as cavemen—was spearheaded by another Victorian named Joseph Knowles who left civilization to live in the wilderness and returned with a model physique; the cabbage soup diet, which gained popularity in the 1980s, has its antecedents in Cato's *De Agri Cultura*—although thankfully the modern version leaves out the urine drinking. *The Blood Type Diet*, popularized by Peter J. D'Adamo in the 1990s, made the outlandish suggestion that different blood groups required different food. And yet it is not so far removed from a theory that persisted until the advance of modern medicine in the 19th century—that we all belong to one of four humors (phlegmatic, choleric, sanguine and melancholic) and that each of them requires a different diet for good health.

However, the last five years have birthed one genuinely new dieting innovation: wellness.

Alternately referred to as clean eating, it's a system that champions unprocessed, additive-free and primarily vegan ingredients, cooked in simple styles or eaten raw. In many ways, it's a return to something sensible and instinctive—the fresh, plant-based diet advocated by the Ancient Greeks. But clean eating can easily become a diet by another name. Laura Thomas, an English nutritionist who describes a diet as "anything that promotes guilt around eating, and any time a set of rigid rules are applied" argues that the regime fits the template of a fad, and is one of a growing number of dietary prescriptions that are cloaking themselves in the language of health and fitness. "We do recognize the damage of fad diets but at the same time we're not recognizing that intentional weight loss is still a diet," she says. "What has changed is what we're calling it and how we're presenting it. We're making it aspirational and a lifestyle. Even companies like Slimming World and Weight Watchers have dropped the 'diet' word because it's not acceptable to people anymore. It's not cool to be on a diet." Where the Victorian diet gurus spoke about scientific breakthroughs to make their case, clean eaters do something similar with the language of nutrition—they talk about toxins, pH levels and how gluten breaks down the microvilli in your gut. "It's presented under the guise of health but a lot of it isn't about health," says Thomas.

So if clean eating is a fad, what will replace it? She predicts that our next obsession will be of a similar stripe—a set of food rules that don't explicitly reference weight loss. "People are going down this route of sustainable eating, which isn't inherently a bad thing—we should all be making better choices for the environment," she says. "But where that becomes problematic is if you've got a broken or troubled relationship with food, and people are saying that you can't eat an avocado because it came from Mexico, or you can only buy your food from the farmers market or food that doesn't come from plastic packaging. People who are prone to embodying food rules will see that as a new standard." Google Trends data shows a steady increase over time in a word that describes people who take healthy dieting to an unhealthy extreme: orthorexia.

I ask Foxcroft for her predictions for the future of fad dieting, but it's not a discussion she's interested in having. "It's all just another turn of the wheel," she tells me. "There's actually a very small pool of dieting advice to plug into, but everybody who is selling a diet will just alter it slightly—they'll use different language or have some appliance that will go with it, or give it a different name."

On one point, the *Calories & Corsets* author is clear. "I wish I'd written a diet book instead of a history book," Foxcroft says, laughing. "I'd be rolling in it by now."

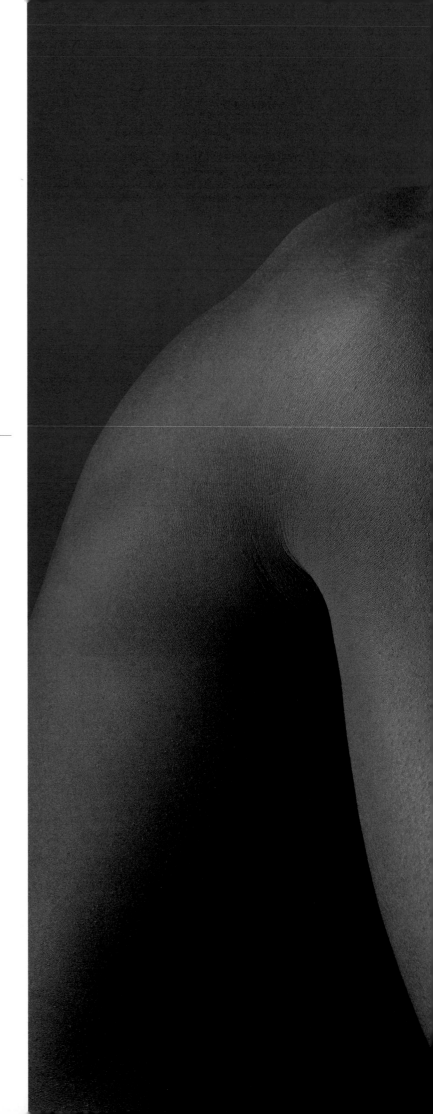

Close Contact

Tactile. Physical. Corporeal: Sport as a liberating force
for the body. Photography by *Jonas Bjerre-Poulsen*

SPORT

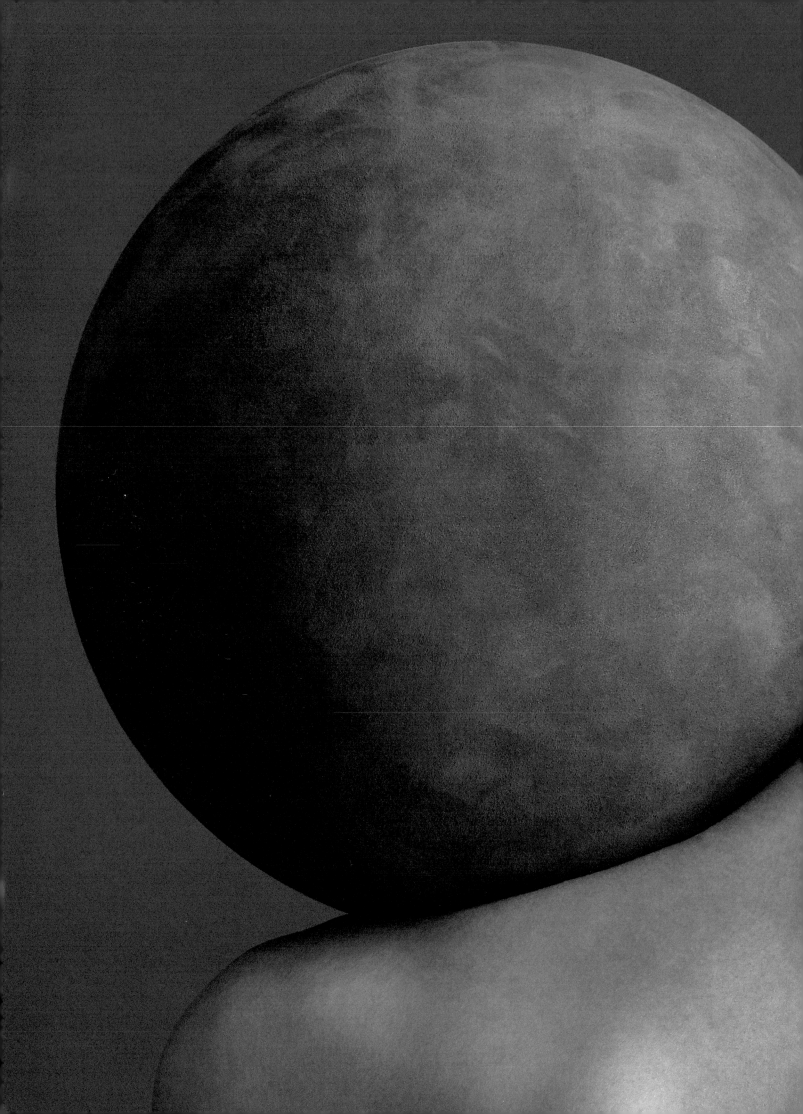

4
Directory

CHARLES SHAFAIEH

Siri Hustvedt

The novelist discusses memory, our need for community and why art matters.

The work of Siri Hustvedt—novelist, critic, poet, and lecturer on psychiatry at Cornell's Weill Medical School—is concerned with imprecision, the discomforting and the unknowable. "There is something alienating about perfection," she writes in her latest book, *A Woman Looking at Men Looking at Women: Essays on Art, Sex, and the Mind.* Many thinkers are intent on ignoring the fact that we are all flawed bodies who forget, grow and change—producing a range of emotions that are never constant because a person's identity is never fixed. Hustvedt however, whether writing on Louise Bourgeois, Pedro Almodóvar or the millennia-old mind/body debate, doesn't lose sight of our limits as a species or our immense powers of self-expression.

Memory and place have an important bond. But are our memory faculties changing as the world becomes increasingly virtual? There has been a longstanding fear that technology will forever alter our ability to retain memories, and it's true that the art of memory isn't what it used to be. Technology, whether the book or computer, changes us, but the question is: To what degree? Chips can now be inserted into people's bodies to enable certain tasks, but how different is this from a blind person's cane becoming part of her body—an extended self? How do we distinguish between new and old technology as tools? What constitutes a tool? And when does a tool become something sinister?

I don't want to underplay the changes technology creates, but technologies have often led to hysterias. "Internet addiction" is not so different from "railway spine"—a 19th-century illness invented because medicine deemed train accidents uniquely horrific. The fear suggests that people blame the technology rather than themselves. Technology is a vehicle, not the agent. What is happening on the internet is caused by human beings.

You've said that you ingest artists into yourself after consuming their work—they become part of you in a way that cannot be clearly demarcated or defined. Is there then a community of people contained within yourself? The self is co-constituted. There is no self without an other, and the idea of community for human beings is not an option. We are born early, retain juvenile characteristics much longer than other mammals, and remain extraordinarily dependent on others for a lifetime. But the fantasy of the autonomous or "self-made man" in the West, rooted in the Protestant Reformation and the Enlightenment, has had pernicious consequences. Alexis de Tocqueville said that Americans cut themselves off from their ancestors, their descendants and their contemporaries. I advocate the recognition of an intersubjective reality through which we find and make ourselves. All works of art contain traces of a living consciousness, and our relation to art is also intersubjective.

Unlike many writers who engage with philosophical subjects, you never forget that humans are bodies that think and live in the world. Why has the body been so discarded? Misogyny. The mind and intellect have always been associated with men and the body with women. Aristotle, who believed that inert matter is the female principle and form/animated spirit is male, codified the division. The problem persists. Descartes' *Meditations* is a work of stunning clarity and beauty, but he actually denies his parentage as essential to his existence. The myth of the self-made man is a denial of origin. Let's be honest: We all originate inside a woman's body!

Is any knowledge or particular experience necessary to enjoy or understand art? Everyone has a visceral experience of art, which is why no one should wear audio guides while looking. The guide will direct your vision and prohibit you seeing anything other than what you're told to see. We cannot see the world or art naked. We always bring our prejudices and pasts to a work. Taking time helps. If a person parks herself in front of a canvas for two hours, even if she doesn't know anything about painting, she will see what she didn't see at the beginning and what she does not expect to see.

What is the purpose of art? Many people go to art to confirm what they already know. A lot of fiction is consumed because it verifies the reader's worldview. That's a cozy feeling. In my daily life, I love routine, but when it comes to art, I hate it.

When art is good, it shakes us up. It takes us out of our everyday perceptual reality and gives us access to experiences that we wouldn't otherwise have, enlarging our consciousness and unconsciousness. With a novel, we can safely have extreme experiences that we would run away from in real life. Standing in front of a painting, we won't necessarily have new feelings, but we can recognize something about our own experience that we couldn't have recognized otherwise.

Art is like sex. If you don't relax, you won't enjoy it. That openness—to the degree that we can be open—is so important. And I think every person who cares about art knows that there are moments in one's life when you simply are not ready for something. Finding meaning in art may also take time.

Hustvedt is the author of a book of poetry, three collections of essays, a work of non-fiction and six novels, including the Man Booker Prize—nominated *The Blazing World*.

Sometimes decadent, often secret, but never just one: the compulsion to collect.

MATT CASTLE

Possession Obsession

Owning a collection presents the need for places in which to store it. Right: A stationery container by Australian design studio Daniel Emma.

The Pre-Raphaelite painter and poet Dante Gabriel Rossetti was an obsessive collector of exotic animals and birds. He filled his London home with owls, armadillos, peacocks, parakeets, kangaroos, wallabies, a Japanese salamander and a wombat named Top, whom he described as "a joy, a triumph, a delight, a madness." The actor Tom Hanks collects vintage typewriters and was famously bribed to appear on a podcast by means of a crimson 1934 Smith Corona portable.

The urge to collect is deeply embedded within the human psyche. By the age of two, most children grasp the idea of ownership and will go on to acquire one or more "attachment objects," whose perceived specialness depends largely on the fact that the objects are theirs, or were theirs first. A study by Bruce Hood and Paul Bloom explored this phenomenon by asking young children to swap their attachment objects with identical duplicates produced from a mocked-up "copying machine." The idea horrified most of the children, with some even refusing to allow their objects to be "copied" in the first place. Others dutifully agreed to the swap, before bursting into tears.

The enhanced value we ascribe to things we own persists into adult life and is pervasive in the western world. It's known as the "endowment effect," but it doesn't explain why people are attracted to certain items in the first place. For some—connoisseurs of sports team memorabilia, for example—the acquisitive urge may originate from a sense of loyalty or identity, before it morphs into the need to reach ever more ambitious collecting goals.

The tendency of collectors to seek groups of objects was examined by Kate Barasz, a former doctoral student at Harvard Business School, and her colleagues. They demonstrated that arbitrary items framed as a set—which they termed a "pseudo-set"—became more attractive to collectors, who would readily pay more for the set than for the same items presented individually. The researchers did add an important proviso: Don't make the pseudo-set too large. The goal should be achievable.

Sometimes, even the most over-the-top collectors learn to recognize the limits of their desire to acquire. When Rossetti's beloved Top expired scant months after coming into his possession, he had the marsupial stuffed and mounted. History records a short-lived replacement—but thereafter, the painter-poet sought no further wombats. The joy and the madness must end somewhere.

JUST YOUR TYPE
by Pip Usher

Of all the things a Hollywood star could choose to blow enormous sums of money on, manual typewriters do not seem an obvious choice. "I probably have 250-plus typewriters in my collection," announces Tom Hanks in *California Typewriter*, a documentary about typewriters that documented his obsession and debuted in August to critical acclaim. Tapping away on a Smith Corona, numerous other models in camel brown, bottle green and gray displayed neatly on shelves behind him, Hanks displays a collector's paternal pride. "I would say that 90 percent of them are in perfect working order," he adds. It's a 40-year-long obsession that started with a humble Hermes 2000—his first investment. "I ended up just having them around because they're beautiful works of art," Hanks told NPR. Since then, he has not only amassed a substantial collection from "every ridiculous source possible," but has translated his passion into the digital age with the launch of Hanx Writer—a best-selling iPad app that recreates the genteel typography and clackety-clack experience of a manual typewriter. Should other purists worry, Hanks' latest tribute takes a more traditional format. In a new collection of short stories, *Uncommon Type*, published in October, Hanks drew 17 different tales together with one common theme: the typewriter.

Bob Ross

Learning the art of relaxation from the master of happy accidents (and accidental life advice).

It is difficult to recall any one Bob Ross painting. *Mountain Waterfall* looks a lot like *Mountain Retreat*, which looks a lot like *Brown Mountain* before it and *Autumn Mountain* before that. As the host of *The Joy of Painting*, an American television tutorial that ran for 31 seasons between 1983 and 1994, Ross painted over 400 variations on the theme. His was an oeuvre of quantity—a prolific series of boreal mirages, like New Age desktop wallpapers. "Talent is a pursued interest," he once said.

Ross (pictured above, holding a baby raccoon) was the first to admit that his paintings comprised lots of what he called "happy accidents." He encouraged viewers to make them too, and not to worry. Mistakes could be turned into trees, and Ross saw all trees as happy and little. "And don't make your trees straight," he advised. "Let them bend. Trees grow in all kinds of ways. Doesn't really matter."

Ross has gathered a wider fan base in death. Meme culture appreciates the perm that he wore like a fur hat and the cameos of Peapod, the pocket squirrel; the ASMR community delights in the bristly tap-tap of his paintbrush and his pronunciation of "wh" as "hw" (hwy, hwere, titanium hwite). Netflix has picked up one of his shows and Target sells a Bob Ross board game.

"We're not sure that he would have imagined that it would have gotten this big," says Joan Kowalski, president at Bob Ross Inc. ("the machine behind the man"). "He was peripherally aware that people could never watch a full episode because they would fall asleep in the middle of it." He would have been shy and flattered, she thinks. "He could just be that wonderful person that everyone saw on television."

The enduring appeal of Bob Ross, Kowalski believes, is the safe space he created to "explore your ability to be creative without having a lot of experience." Perhaps it is also that any viewer can adapt his wet-on-wet painting techniques into solid life advice. For example: "If you don't like it, change it. It's your world."

Corralled in the Chihuahuan Desert, Donald Judd's library has its own ecosystem.

MOLLY MANDELL

Cult Rooms

The artist Donald Judd had admirers so passionate that, following his death in 1994, they created bumper stickers and T-shirts emblazoned with "WWDJD"—an acronym for "What would Donald Judd do?"

Perhaps a better question would have been, "What would Donald Judd *read*?" Unbeknownst to many, Judd was an avid bibliophile. His passion for books culminated in a library in the west Texas town of Marfa, an unlikely destination that has since become a hotbed for the arts as a result of Judd's influence and work.

Judd first visited Marfa as a soldier in December 1946 and the landscape captivated him so much that he sent a telegram to his mother about it. Before he settled there 26 years later, in 1972, Judd had become an influential member of the New York art world, both as a critic and as an artist. Eventually rejecting the New York scene as "glib and harsh," he resolved to find a new place for his art. After considering multiple towns in southwest Texas, Judd chose Marfa because it was the "best looking and most practical."

Until his death, Judd invested almost all his money in the town. Over time, he acquired two aircraft hangars, a former cavalry base, a bank, more than 40,000 acres of land, a defunct grocery store, a hotel, six homes, several commercial buildings and the local hot springs. He also built a library to house his collection of nearly 13,000 books.

"Don believed that you should have a lifelong relationship with books and always question the world around you," says Judd's daughter, Rainer. She fondly remembers purchasing books with her father. "We bought a lot of books on our travels, and always shipped them back to Marfa. Back in Marfa, if you weren't careful, you would find that Don had taken your books. He thought that every book was interesting in some way." It was this conviction that drove him to amass a library spanning 40 languages and 576 shelves.

Judd had very fixed ideas about the organization of his library and personally catalogued his inventory (this detail is perhaps unsurprising given he also held notoriously strong views about how and where his artwork should be displayed). Judd's collections were split between pre-20th and 20th-century topics. The first was organized by country and the latter by subject matter. "Within the arts and architecture section, Don arranged the books by artists' or architects' birth dates," says Rainer. "He also created lists, a few of which are still on the shelves, of artists' birth and death dates."

Thousands of people make the pilgrimage to Marfa each year, many of whom are interested in getting a glimpse into the seminal artist's legacy. Judd Foundation, which is run by Rainer and her brother, Flavin, preserves Judd's studios, offices and private residence in the town. Perhaps most importantly, the foundation preserves his library.

"Don was always interested in the writers who lived and worked in the cities and countries that we traveled to," says Rainer. "He felt it was important to understand the context and history of these places and the people who lived there." For those traveling to Marfa, Judd's vast collection of books is arguably the best way to get to know the artist and the town that he reinvigorated. *Photography by Elizabeth Felicella*

Judd wrote on a broad range of topics. In 2016, Judd Foundation and David Zwirner Books published *Donald Judd Writing* — a collection of the artist's essays, notes and manuscripts from 1958 to 1993.

SELECTED READING
by Molly Mandell

Donald Judd's library offers an insight into just how varied his interests were. Of the 13,000 books in his collection, 3,129 focus on art. The artist was known for having duplicates so that he could lend or give away his favorite books: He owned not one but four copies of *Cacti of the Southwest*, published by the University of Texas Press. "Dozens of periodicals and books on cacti and succulents can be found in Judd's library," says Caitlin Murray, an archivist and director of programs at Judd Foundation. "He planted and maintained his own cacti garden at The Block [his residence in Marfa]." Murray also identifies the writings of Italian political philosopher and rhetorician Giambattista Vico as an integral part of Judd's collection. In one personal note dated August 28, 1985, Judd calls Vico a "man to admire." Lastly, Murray points to another of Judd's favorites, *Small is Beautiful: A Study of Economics as if People Mattered*—a critique of Western economic models.

Hermione Skye

Modern projects, ancient philosophy: The creative director of Wakimukudo The Label explains her ethos.

From a studio in the UK and another in Japan, Wakimukudo The Label designs meditation rooms and patterns, crafts loom installations and curates Japanese teahouses. Their portfolio presents a patchwork of projects woven together with a single, panoptic thread. Every work of art is *wakimukudo*, a term compounded from several Japanese words, including those translating to harmony, energy and way of being. This one melodic expression represents a positive, humble stimulus that triggers a feeling of contentment and satisfaction. Hermione Skye, the label's creative director, has discovered wakimukudo is a pleasure worth bringing home at the end of a workday.

Can you walk us through your creative process? We believe that although the clock keeps ticking, most true wisdom was found in the days of antiquities, particularly in Japan. The beauty that resonates most with the ancient understandings is found in the simple and underappreciated. Art and aesthetics don't simply please a setting or visual-cognitive brain pathways; they capture the heart. In the UK, light reflected on the water provokes loom installations and teahouse projects. The shape and movement inspire me to grasp what the eyes cannot detect but what the heart feels—that feeling of wakimukudo. It's a light and positive feeling within one's chest.

What's an average day like for you? There isn't an average day. Nevertheless, most days consist of creating the blueprints of our signature loom installations and ground murals. Ancient Japanese battle formations are often inspiration. Although samurais used them to shape armies, the formations reflect a true understanding of life's continuous flow and impermanence. My day might entail flipping through tattered old books about Japanese battle strategy and geometry, adapting them to a contemporary setting. But don't expect to find me eating at my desk. I still work closely with our team in Japan, where we seek inspiration in temples during our lunch hour.

Why is it so important to adapt ancient techniques or aesthetics for a contemporary context? There has been so much negative propaganda that utilizes an understanding of how the brain works, masking a stimulus and priming it within the subconscious. This creates unconscious alterations in thought patterns and even actions. On the other hand, ancient or traditional artistic aesthetics use wisdom that enables individuals to find positivity within themselves, which is then confirmed by wakimukudo. I work very closely with my cofounders, who are cognitive neuroscientists.

Is there a motto that Wakimukudo The Label works by? Our motto is "never a replica of an existing thought." We will never recreate a room installation, teahouse, or even website design. Like life and energy, our designs are continuously evolving. We don't believe in stagnancy.

What attracts your clients to Wakimukudo The Label? Our typical clients range from individuals in the banking industry who crave a meditation space in a modern apartment building, to holistic instructors, dieticians, and even hotels, cafes, and spas. They're attracted to both Wakimukudo The Label's modernity and traditionalism. Today, there's such a strong division between our hearts and minds that we're numb to ourselves. Our clients appreciate the traditional, simple and nostalgic designs that reestablish a pathway to the heart.

With offices on two continents, how would you describe your team? All of our team members follow tradition, not only in our designs but also with our actions, interactions and speech. On both continents, we are people of the heart. Our team leader in Japan is a senior tea master. Although the tea ceremony is a way of being, she also performs it to come up with new ideas and teahouse curations. Interestingly, she says that when one does a tea ceremony for oneself, the water's movement creates a flow between the heart and mind.

Does working between the UK and Japan present any challenges? Other than the time difference, I don't find any challenges. Only benefits. I studied interior temple design in Japan for over a year, which required disciplining my thoughts and way of being. I've come to appreciate how the team in Japan finds beauty in simplicity. Their patience and humility are traditional philosophies that I continuously strive for. Wakimukudo is a way of being for all of us, but it's also a daily challenge to design a positive stimulus felt within the heart and triggered by nostalgia for unseen realities.

What sets the label apart from other design houses? Design houses in the UK function more as rigid businesses. Often, they follow a client's taste to make an area look "Instagram approved." For us, design and curation are ways of being, and a way of disciplining and perfecting ourselves. It's the same as the tea master who continues practicing the way of tea until the day she leaves the physical world. Even in something as simple as interior design, we respect every object and every person we work with. They are part of the overall design. And these designs are similar to a cup of tea in a traditional Japanese tea ceremony, a sign of appreciation to the guests and surroundings. If you look closely, you'll notice that a signature Wakimukudo The Label design always has a small space or part that is "unfinished." That's a way for us to pay respect to fate, destiny and the surprises that the universe presents when one is true to the way of the heart.
—
This feature is produced in partnership with Wakimukudo The Label.

Eleven clues in this anatomy-themed puzzle are trying tibia little humerus.

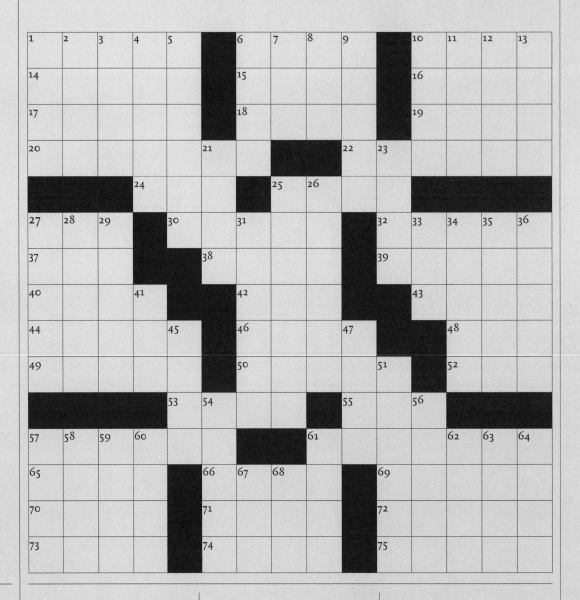

MOLLY YOUNG

Crossword

ACROSS

1. *Popular orange variety
6. *Baby bovine
10. *Something to hit with a hammer
14. Dramatic device
15. "Splendor in the Grass" director Kazan
16. Nullify
17. Powdery purple hue
18. Connection
19. What may form in your hair if you neglect to brush it
20. Shoulder bag
22. Lofty principles
24. English Breakfast or Assam, for example
25. Indian attire
27. *Provide with weaponry
30. Mistake
32. Range
37. Expire
38. Actor, director, writer and activist Dunham
39. Nobel-winning author of "The Stranger"

40. Unsightly
42. Tavern
43. Helpful hints
44. Where to wear earrings
46. Salt Lake City state
48. "Aunt" in Spanish
49. Rubbish
50. Deadly
52. Sneaky
53. Clumsy ones
55. *Cool
57. *Weaver in Shakespeare's "A Midsummer Night's Dream"
61. Tropical yellow fruits that are actually berries
65. Region
66. René Redzepi restaurant in Copenhagen, Denmark
69. Candied, as fruits
70. Bring to market
71. *Bearded purple flower
72. Darkest part of a shadow
73. *Mild white fish
74. Curse
75. Valuable possession

DOWN

1. Scandinavian version of the name "Nicholas"
2. Opera solo
3. Electrical unit
4. Make into law
5. Small, fragrant fruit with white flesh and red skin
6. *Room in a prison
7. Boxing great Muhammad
8. "Hamilton" creator
9. Sufi ascetic
10. Pop in the microwave, slangily
11. Leo Tolsoy's "____ Karenina"
12. One to revere
13. Tons
21. British nobleman
23. Frisbee shape
25. Many Mozart compositions
26. Biblical mountain
27. Grown-up
28. Discipline
29. Type of toast
31. Snub
33. Leopard or puma (e.g.)

34. Leaves out
35. *Student
36. Prose form popularized by Montaigne
41. Affirmative answer
45. Drive away
47. "Very funny"
51. ____ franca
54. Prenatal test, for short
56. *Desert island trees
57. Chorus member with a low voice
58. Classic black-and-white sandwich cookie
59. Tattle
60. Story
61. Party, slangily
62. Catches
63. Unit of farmland
64. Chair
67. Singer Rita
68. "With" in German

Andrea Codrington Lippke

Design journalist and *Kinfolk* contributing editor *Andrea Codrington Lippke* on the most and least beneficial of her personal habits.

Illustration: Chidy Wayne

What is one bad habit you wish you could give up?
Comparing myself to others. Relentlessly.
What is one good habit you're proud of and how did you establish it?
Making sure that every night I kiss my husband goodnight and tell him that I love him. Especially if I'm angry. Practice makes perfect.
What is one piece of information you wish you could unlearn?
My mother told me once that when they were young she and my father would squeeze lime juice on each other's skin after a day at the beach and lick it off. Need I say more?

WINTER 2018

www.apuntob.it

Stockists

ACNE STUDIOS
acnestudios.com

ALESSI
alessi.com

ALISON JACKSON
alisonjackson.com

ANDERSON & SHEPPARD
anderson-sheppard.co.uk

APUNTOB
apuntob.com

BASSIKE
bassike.com

BELSTAFF
belstaff.co.uk

BOLLINGER
bollingerfitness.com

BRAUN
braun.com

BREELAYNE
breelayne.com

BRUNELLO CUCINELLI
brunellocucinelli.com

BUDD
buddshirts.co.uk

CANALI
canali.com

CARTIER
cartier.com

CASIO
casio.com

CÉLINE
celine.com

COCLICO
coclico.com

DANIEL EMMA
daniel-emma.com

DSQUARED2
dsquared2.com

ERMANNO SCERVINO
ermannoscervino.it

FARIS
farisfaris.com

FREYA DALSJØ
freyadalsjo.com

GUCCI
gucci.com

HAY
hay.dk

HELBERS
helbers.fr

HERMÈS
hermes.com

HOCK
hockdesign.com

IITTALA
iittala.com

JACQUEMUS
jacquemus.com

JW ANDERSON
j-w-anderson.com

LEVI'S
levi.com

LOEWE
loewe.com

LUCCHESE
lucchese.com

LUISAVIAROMA
luisaviaroma.com

MAISON MARGIELA
maisonmargiela.com

MARGARET HOWELL
margarethowell.co.uk

MARK KENLY DOMINO TAN
markkenlydominotan.com

MARQUES ALMEIDA
marquesalmeida.com

MONCLER
moncler.com

MULBERRY
mulberry.com

NEIL BARRETT
neilbarrett.com

ORLEBAR BROWN
orlebarbrown.com

OUTDOOR VOICES
outdoorvoices.com

PALOMA WOOL
palomawool.com

PARI DESAI
paridesai.com

PAULA MENDOZA
paulamendoza.com

PRINGLE OF SCOTLAND
pringlescotland.com

RAINS
rains.com

SCHOOLHOUSE
schoolhouse.com

SHAINA MOTE
shainamote.com

SONIA RYKIEL
soniarykiel.com

STRING
string.se

SUNDANCE RESORT
sundanceresort.com

SUNSPEL
sunspel.com

SØRENSEN LEATHER
sorensenleather.com

TINA FREY
tinafreydesigns.com

TINGEST
tingest.se

URBANEARS
urbanears.com

WAKIMUKUDO
wakimukudothelabel.com

Z ZEGNA
zegna.co.uk

COCLICO

COCLICO.COM

CONSCIOUSLY   ARTFULLY   ELEGANTLY

ISSUE 26

Credits

P. 24
Jacket by *Mark Kenly Domino Tan*. Special thanks to Menu Space

P. 27
Model
Giannina Oteto

P. 70-81
Courtesy of and copyright *The Gordon Parks Foundation*

P. 82-95
Production
Kim Hallsworth

Grooming
Lyz Marsden

Model
Olivier at Nevs Models

Photography Assistants
Jakub Gloser
Adam Lang

P. 114-129
Production
Samuel Åberg

Hair and Makeup
Rebecca Rojas

Photography Assistant
Thomas Alexander

Digital Operator
Nick Martin

P. 130-133
This essay originally appeared in the June 30, 2014 issue of *The New Yorker* and is published with the permission of the author. © 2014 by *David Sedaris*

P. 144-161
Set Design
Joanna Goodman

Production
Samuel Åberg

Grooming
Mike O'Gorman

Models
Dennis at AMCK Models
Luke at Established Models

Casting Director
Sarah Bunter

Photography Assistants
Nick Martin
Mike Mills

Set Design Assistant
Grace Manning

P.181
Bob Ross name and images are registered trademarks of Bob Ross Inc. © Bob Ross Inc. All Rights Reserved. Used with permission.

P. 182
South Library, La Mansana de Chinati/The Block, Judd Foundation, Marfa, Texas © Judd Foundation

P. 184-185
Photography
Gabby Laurent

Hair & Makeup
Louisa Copperwaite

Photography Assistant
Kerimcan Goren

Special Thanks
Mario Depicolzuane
Karen Hagen
Djassi Johnson
Paul Lukas
Manal Mufrrej
Sorensen Leather
Duncan Will